PUCK SHY

TEAGAN HUNTER

Editing by Editing by C. Marie

Proofreading by Judy's Proofreading & Julia Griffis

Cover Design: Emily Wittig Designs

To hockey butts.
Thanks for existing.

CHAPTER 1

COLLIN

"No, no, no…"

Smoke billows from under the hood of my old beat-up Land Cruiser that has certainly seen better days. With a groan, I navigate it onto the shoulder, and just as I get the last tire off the main road, the car dies completely.

Dread sinks into my gut.

I'm more capable of handling a hockey stick than a wrench, but even I know smoke like this isn't a good sign.

I sigh and yank up the emergency brake, then slam my hand against the steering wheel in frustration. I've already been stranded in a podunk town for two days while I had to wait on new tires to be delivered to replace my two popped ones.

Now, less than four hours from home, I'm fucked again.

I knew driving the old beater vehicle across the country probably wasn't the best idea. I should have listened to my pops when he suggested I flatbed it. He knew the car wouldn't make the trek from the middle of nowhere Kansas all the way to North Carolina.

I was determined to have the last few days of my break to myself though. Just me and the open road, nothing but my thoughts to keep me company.

Turns out that was a bad idea too because my thoughts suck as much as this car does.

The end of last season has been on perpetual repeat in my brain, and I've spent the entire drive thinking of all the things I could have done differently to not cost us the Stanley Cup.

Such as not taking a penalty just moments before the end of the tied regulation, which led to a goal *and* the loss of Game Six in overtime. After we won Game One, we were feeling good, ready to take it to the end. But after losing Games Two, Three, and Four—in overtime, no less—we were feeling defeated. We rallied for Game Five and barely scraped by with a win, but that spark was back. Then Game Six happened and we folded like a house of cards at the last minute, blowing the series.

It was a total punch to the heart.

I wish I could say that was the worst of it for me.

A car speeds by, shaking the SUV and pulling me from recalling one of the worst moments of my life.

I don't need to take a trip down memory lane. Right now, I need to figure out what the hell I'm going to do to get back home. Coach expects the team to report tomorrow at 8 AM, and after letting him down last season, I can't be late. This year *has* to go better than last.

I have a contract on the line. I need to get my shit together, prove I'm worth the time and money. I want to stay with the Comets, and I'll do whatever it takes to make that happen.

I pop the hood and hop out of the car to take a look at the damage.

When I peer in at the engine, it's obvious I'm not going anywhere anytime soon. There's errant fluid, and a low hiss echoes on the otherwise quiet road; it's coming from around where the smoke is rising.

A tow is definitely in order.

I wipe my hands off on my jeans—something my mom would kill me for if she saw me—and round the car to grab my phone from the cup holder.

I search for the nearest mechanic and hit GO on the results.

And I wait.

Then wait some more.

Nothing.

There's not enough service to get the results to load.

I walk up and down the road, but it's no use. I'm in the middle of nowhere. There's nothing for miles.

With my frustration growing, I trek back to my car and survey the area. I'm not sure what I'm looking for. A rescue maybe? I didn't pass many cars when driving, so I'm not expecting anyone to come flying down the road anytime soon.

I'm about an hour and a half from sunset, maybe less, and I think there was an exit about five or so miles back. If I hustle, I can probably make it before it gets too dark out.

"Fuck it," I mutter to nobody but myself. "I'll walk."

Hell, maybe it'll be good for me. Help clear my head.

I grab my wallet from the center console and a flashlight out of the glovebox just in case I need it, then lock up the car.

I shoot off a text to Rhodes, the one guy on the team who doesn't want to choke the shit out of me, hoping it'll go through eventually and he can send someone to help.

I slip my phone into my back pocket and, somehow —despite having done it a hundred times before—I miss.

The overpriced hunk of metal crashes to the ground. I don't even have to pick it up to know the screen is shattered because that's just the kind of luck I have lately.

Not that I give a shit about the phone being broken. I can buy another with no problem.

My issue is that everything that could possibly go wrong since blowing the Cup has gone wrong.

The week after we lost, a few guys from the team— the ones still talking to me—got together at a local bar to drown our sorrows. After one too many drinks were slung around, a brawl ensued after I witnessed some asshole manhandling a woman.

I did the right thing. I stepped in and handled shit.

But guess who got slapped with the cuffs after it was all said and done?

Me. That's fucking who.

Luckily the asshole ended up dropping the charges when the truth about what started the fight came out.

The damage was done though. I was branded a hothead when the press began digging into my past, and a file that should have been clean suddenly wasn't.

Two arrests for assault? Not a good look on the team.

With my name and face being splashed across headlines and social media, Coach suggested I lie low for the summer, get my head on straight before the upcoming season. So, I packed my bag and headed out west to my parents' farm.

The flight out to my parents' house? Rescheduled... twice. To top it off, my luggage was lost, and I ended up having to wear my brother's too-small clothes the first three days I was there.

Mom forgot to mention she turned my old bedroom into an office, so I crashed on the same lumpy, uncomfortable couch we've had since I was in middle school. At six foot three, the couch is the last place I need to be sleeping. That first week home was spent with a kink in my neck, and I swear it's still fucked up.

That was just the beginning of the shitstorm that would follow.

I thought going back home for the summer would be good for me, thought being away from the city I let down would be for the best. I could put the loss and the gossip behind me and get my mind right. But everything that could go wrong did, and the more shit went wrong, the more I couldn't help but think it was all my fault somehow.

I pinch my nose between my fingers, inhaling and exhaling slowly to remain calm.

Figuring shit out under pressure isn't typically a problem for me. You don't become a first-round draft pick in the NHL by not being able to handle the heat.

But today, my ability to stay cool is being tested beyond belief.

First my car, now my phone.

"Can't just *one* thing go right for a change?"

With a huff, I snatch my phone off the ground to assess the damage.

As expected, the screen is toast. But the real kick in the nuts?

It won't turn on.

"Just fucking great." Now if my text did somehow go through to Rhodes, he's not going to have any way to get ahold of me.

Fury races through me and I want nothing more than to smash the useless device against a tree, but I refrain.

Instead, I set off down the road again, keeping my head down, making sure to stay far away from the two-lane highway. The sky grows darker a lot faster than I anticipated, and I've misjudged either how long I have until sundown or how far back this exit is.

I walk about a mile before I see headlights pop over a hill in the distance. Whoever it is, they're flying.

And that worries me because the closer they creep to the edge of the road, the closer they're getting to me.

Does the universe hate me so much that I'm about to get mowed down in the middle of nowhere with nobody to witness it? Where they likely wouldn't find my body for days?

The driver isn't showing any sign of slowing or moving over.

I slow my gait as they approach, ready to jump out of the way if I have to. And I really fucking think I'm going to have to.

Just when I'm sure I'm going to have to dive into the ditch for safety, a loud squeal pierces the air as they slam on their brakes, fishtailing all over the road.

The car skids another thirty yards or so before coming to a complete stop.

I'm paralyzed.

I can't move. Can't look away from the car that's now just sitting in the middle of the road.

What the hell just happened?

The sky is still bright enough that I can see the driver's form in the car. Can see them sitting there unmoving, likely in the same state of shock I'm in.

Finally, they shake their head and ease their foot off the brake.

Are they just going to drive away? After they almost hit me? Just like fucking that?

I take two steps toward the vehicle, ready to—*fuck*, I don't even know what I'm going to do. Yell at them?

Chase them down? That'd be stupid. Plus, I don't need to get in any more trouble than I'm already in.

But I'm *pissed*. Who almost hits a person, then just drives off like it's nothing?

I stop walking when the car slowly eases onto the shoulder and the driver kills the engine.

Guess they are going to stop after all.

I wait for whoever it is to make the first move. To roll down the window and ask if I'm okay. To get out and apologize. To do anything other than sit there. It's too dark to see into the car completely, but I can feel them staring at me in the rearview mirror.

I stare back, my anger growing by the second.

I swear it's hours before the door finally pops open.

"What the hell is your problem?" I lay into them the moment the door is ajar. "Do you have any idea how close you were to hitting me? You could have kil—"

I try to rein in my surprise when a woman who can't be more than five foot five steps out of the car and turns to face me.

She shoves long, wavy strands of hair out of her face. She's still a good twenty feet away, but I can see the shock in her eyes from here. Her jaw is dropped, hands shaking at her sides.

She takes a step toward me. Then another.

She stops at the back of her car and stares at me with wide eyes.

But it's not the same wide-eyed stare I get from fans. There's no sign of recognition on her face.

She looks terrified out of her mind. Like she's scared of me.

Ridiculous considering I'm the one who almost got dead.

We stare at one another for several beats, not saying a peep. It's calm out here, not much of a breeze. Nothing to fill the silence between us except her quiet breaths.

I don't know what the etiquette is here. Just moments ago I was ready to lay into her, but the look she's giving me…

"I, uh…"

A pause.

Ten seconds pass.

"I…" She tries again, her tongue darting out to wet her lips. She pulls the bottom one between her teeth, trapping it there while she mulls over what she's going to say next.

A sigh.

And finally, "Are you okay?"

Her voice is soft. Timid.

I nod.

"I…I didn't see you. And then I did. But I thought… I thought you weren't real."

I tilt my head. "Not real?"

My voice comes out gruffer than I intend, probably from not talking to anyone for so long. She looks as surprised as I do by the sound of it.

"You know, the stories about this road. I thought you were the Ghostly Drifter."

9

"Ghostly Drifter?"

I have no fucking clue why I'm just repeating the ends of her sentences.

She doesn't seem to mind.

"You haven't heard the stories?"

I shake my head.

She wrings her hands, eyes darting around, taking in the heavily wooded area around us. "Well, supposedly, along this stretch of highway, a drifter roams. He's said to show up around dusk, and he only appears to people who are alone. He flags you down, claiming his car broke down, and asks for a ride. If you let him into your car, you're giving him permission."

"Permission for what?"

"To eat your soul. It's said he absorbs all the good parts of you, leaving all the bad behind. Everyone who has reported picking him up has committed a horrific crime in the weeks following."

"That…sounds like a load of shit."

She huffs out a laugh. "But I've never seen anyone wandering these roads before tonight, and well…" She lifts her shoulders. "Freaked me out. Probably because I was listening to *Strange, Dark, and Mysterious*."

"You listen to Johnny?"

Her eyes widen with shock and she grins. "You're a fan of the podcast?"

"I listen to him all the time during…" I pause, not wanting to reveal too much about who I am. I have no idea who this woman is. She's not showing any signs of recognizing me, but she could be playing me. It wouldn't be the first time it's happened. "When I'm on a plane," I finish.

"Fly a lot?"

"Sometimes more than I'd like."

Silence falls between us again, and she's back to wringing her hands. She's nervous, but I can't tell if it's me making her feel that way or that we both just almost experienced a life-altering thing.

"I...I really am sorry," she says quietly. Her voice is barely above a whisper, but it carries over to me with ease.

I'm just now realizing how quiet this stretch of the road really is. And after her story—even though it's total bullshit—it's kind of creepy being out here.

"What are you doing out here?"

"My car broke down."

A soft squeak leaves her lips, and I can't help but chuckle.

"I'm not the drifter guy, I promise."

Her eyes narrow. "That sounds exactly like what he'd say."

"Well, I guess the only way you'll know is to let me into your car."

Her face falls, and she takes a step back from me.

"Fuck." I lift the backward cap on my head, running a hand through my hair before replacing it. "That sounded creepy as shit, didn't it?"

She nods.

"Look," I say, taking a step toward her. She steps back again, and I pause, realizing I'm likely scaring the crap out of her right now. "I've been on the road since six this morning, and now my car is broken down. I tried calling for a tow truck but lost signal. Then I dropped my phone, and because nothing these days is made like it once was, it's broken. So now I'm stranded. I saw an exit a couple of miles back and was walking that way when I almost got run over."

She grimaces, her face telling me she's sorry for that.

"It's just been a long day," I tell her. "I'm tired and frustrated and just want to get where I'm going so I can crash. So thanks for not hitting me. I'm fine. You're fine." I toss my thumb over my shoulder. "I'm going to get going before I lose any more light."

I turn on my heel and shove my hands into my pockets, keeping my head up just in case someone else decides to come barreling down the hill and almost kill me.

What a fucking day.

And now I'm going to be out here in the pitch dark.

Fuck do I hope my flashlight doesn't give out on me.

"Wait!"

I hear the crunch of gravel under her shoes as she gets closer.

I spin back around, waiting.

"I…" She sighs. "That exit you saw? That's at least fifteen miles back."

"What? Are you sure?" I could have sworn it wasn't more than two miles.

But everything out here does look the same...

She nods. "I've driven this road a hundred times. It's the exit for Springsville. The next exit that way"—she points the way she was heading—"is another ten miles." She drops her hand, tucking it into her back pocket and rocking back on her heels. "We're in a really rural area, and the cell service is notorious for being nonexistent. You picked a really bad place to break down."

Awesome. Good to know I was walking in the wrong direction.

"Where are you headed?"

It's on the tip of my tongue to tell her, but I don't think that would be the smartest thing to do. For all I know, *she* could be the Ghostly Drifter.

Don't be an idiot, Col. There's no such thing as ghosts.

"Near Jonesville," I say instead. It's not exactly where I'm going, but it's a town over.

"I'm headed to Bartlett. That's on my way..."

Is she... "Are you offering to give me a ride all the way there?"

She shrugs. "I *did* almost run you over. It only seems right."

"I could be dangerous."

She tips her head to the side, watching me closely.

I can't clearly see the color of her eyes from here, but I'm betting it's something brilliant.

"I don't think you are."

I'm not, but… "You don't know me."

"Are you trying to convince me that you *are* dangerous?"

"No. I just think that since—"

"I'm a woman, I'm helpless and incapable of handling myself?" She crosses her arms over her chest, cocking her hip out. She stares at me with hard eyes. "I have a gun in my glovebox."

She looks so tough right now, like she isn't going to take this from me. I like that she's standing up for herself, but still… "I wasn't going to say that. But also, you shouldn't tell me where you keep your weapon."

She tucks her lips together. "That's fair. Though I could be lying about it…"

I get the feeling she's not.

"Do you want a ride or not?"

I really hate that she's offering a ride to a complete stranger, but I'm glad the complete stranger is me.

"It's a Sunday," she says. "Repair shops are going to be closed. What are you going to do? Try to hang around some place until someone can come get you?"

Hanging around in public for hours doesn't sound appealing. I have no fucking clue where I am and now no phone to get ahold of someone.

"All right," I agree. "A ride would be great. I can call for a tow later."

She gives me a single nod and heads for the car.

We make it four steps before she whirls around again.

This time I'm much closer to her, the closest I've been yet.

Her eyes are bright blue, so bright they're almost white. Her lips are pouty and full, the bottom one just slightly larger than the top. Her nose is small and upturned at the end, but not in a distracting way. It's...cute.

She's *cute*.

"What's your name?"

"Huh?" I draw my eyes away from her mouth, back to her eyes that are trained on me with caution.

"Your name?"

"It's...Collin."

"Why didn't you sound sure of that? Is that a fake name?"

"It's not." I'm just not entirely used to someone not knowing who I am. "My name is Collin. My friends call me Col." I leave out my last name on purpose.

"Collin." She tests my name on her lips, like she's trying to decide if she likes it or not. She sticks her hand out to me. "Harper."

"Nice to meet you, Harper." I take her hand in mine, noting how small it is compared to my giant paws. Her skin is soft too. "Thank you for not running me over."

A grin pulls at the corner of her lips. "Come on. We still have about a four-hour drive ahead of us."

"Uh, should I drive? I'm not entirely sure I trust your night vision."

Those white-blue eyes narrow. "Gun, remember?"

"Right, in the glovebox. I remember."

She turns on her heel, making her way to the driver's side of the little white Honda.

That's when I spot it.

A Carolina Comets bumper sticker.

Fuck me.

She really didn't seem like she recognized me at all, but maybe she's just a really good actress? I have nothing to base that on. I don't know her. Which makes me even more of an idiot for willingly getting into the car with her.

She must notice me hesitating.

"Are you memorizing my license plate?"

I already did. "No. I, uh, noticed the sticker. Hockey fan?"

She lets out a single laugh. "No. Not into sports at all. It came with the car." She lifts her shoulders. "Are you?"

"You could say I'm a fan."

"Oh great." She rolls her eyes as I make my way to the passenger door. "Just please don't talk my ear off about it the entire drive or I'm likely to fall asleep at the wheel."

This is going to be a long four hours.

CHAPTER 2

HARPER

You never realize how long a mile is until you're sitting in silence with a stranger you just almost hit with your car.

I am now well aware of just how much it feels like forever as the quiet stretches between us.

Holy shit. I can't believe I almost hit someone.

I *really* can't believe that same someone is now sitting in my passenger seat.

And I lied to him.

There's no such thing as the Ghostly Drifter.

I was totally screwing around with my stereo, trying to get my auxiliary cord to sit right so my podcast would stop cutting out. But making up some story felt better than admitting I was one of those assholes who play with their phone while they're driving.

I steal a glance over at him.

He's tall, so tall that when he folded himself into the car, his knees were against the dash. He leaned the seat back so his head wasn't brushing the ceiling too. His shoulders are wide, and he's taking up every inch of his side of the car and some of mine.

He's turned his baseball cap forward, and I'm a little disappointed by the way it covers his eyes. They're a bright green, and I'm sad I won't ever get to see them in the daylight because I'm betting the color is gorgeous.

His hands are big too as they rest on his jean-clad thighs. They're veiny, but not in that way that's *too* veiny. More in the way that a nurse would look at hands and think, *Wow. That's some serious nurse porn right there.*

I'm trapped in this car with this gorgeous man who smells like leather and something else I can't quite place my finger on.

He's sitting so still it's making me uncomfortable.

"So, how far up here is your car?" I shift around, trying to make conversation.

"I think a mile or so. Do you mind if we stop at it real quick? I need to grab my bags." He huffs out a laugh that contains zero humor. "I really thought I was going to be able to walk to a service station or something and get this taken care of tonight, but that's clearly not going to happen."

It really wasn't.

I didn't lie when I told him we're practically in a dead zone for cell service.

I've driven through these parts enough times in the last three years to know that. I just came from spending the weekend at my mom's to celebrate my sister's engagement to her lawyer fiancé.

Something my mom made sure to bring up every second of the trip.

"I just don't understand why you don't settle down, Harper."

"You should find a successful man like your sister, Harper."

"You're scaring off suitors with all those creepy things you make, Harper."

She means well. I know she does.

But when you watch your parents love each other for sixteen years and then discover that the reason your father died suddenly in a car crash was because he was on his way to visit his mistress...

Well, it kind of screws with you and puts you off relationships.

"Are you from around here?" Collin's deep rumble pulls me from my thoughts.

"Sort of. I'm from Howardsville, but I've lived in Bartlett since I graduated college."

"What's with all the *villes* in this area? I swear every city ends in *ville*."

I laugh. "I thought I was the only person who ever noticed that. It drives me nuts. It's confusing." I glance at him. "Are you from here?"

He takes his time answering but finally says, "No. I'm from Kansas."

"Really? What are you doing all the way out here?"

"Work." He doesn't elaborate, just points up the road. "My car is just over this hill."

A wave of relief flows through me when we reach the top and it's sitting on the side of the road.

At least he wasn't lying about being stranded. That makes me feel marginally better about letting a strange man into my car.

I wasn't lying when I said he doesn't seem like the dangerous type. Maybe that's just me being hopeful and naive, but I'm generally good at reading people.

I pull to a stop behind his SUV. It's not as nice as I expected it to be. He's only wearing a pair of jeans and a t-shirt, but even I have enough fashion sense to see that neither item cost less than a hundred dollars.

Which is insane. I think my entire outfit cost me ten. I love a good clearance rack.

"I'll be right back," he says quietly, but he doesn't make any move to exit the car.

I glance over to find him staring at me expectantly, like he's waiting for confirmation that I'm not going to leave him on the side of the road or something.

"I'll be here," I say reassuringly, trying to pretend I don't love the way the dome light casts shadows across his face. I kill the engine to prove to him I'm not going to leave.

He gives me a single nod, then pushes the door open. He jogs to the vehicle and opens the back door. There's not much, a few bags.

One of them is massive and looks like it weighs nearly half of me, but he slings it over his shoulder with zero apparent effort.

He grabs the other two, then pushes the back door closed with his elbow.

I pop my trunk and climb out of the car to meet him.

He's staring down at the Carolina Comets sticker on the bumper, and I wonder if I offended him by not being a fan of hockey. It's not like I'm anti-sports or anything, they just don't exactly get my nipples hard.

I pause just as I'm about to lift the trunk, remembering what I have in there. I pin him with a glare that I hope is fierce. "Do not judge me for the contents of my trunk."

"As long as it's not a body, I think we're good."

When I wince—because it's not a body per se—he arches a dark brow but doesn't say anything.

Huh. Awfully trusting.

I lift the trunk and hold my breath, waiting for his reaction.

He laughs, and it's a deep, throaty sound that I'm going to pretend I don't find attractive.

"Hey! I said not to judge me."

"I didn't promise not to." He slides his eyes toward my trunk. "You going to move these creepy-as-fuck things or what?"

"They are not creepy!" I reach into the trunk to grab a box of dolls to move to the backseat. "Well, fine. They are kind of creepy. But that's the point of them."

"Please tell me you don't collect these."

"For personal use? No. But I do use them to make decor."

"You...make stuff with these?"

I nod as I pull open the back passenger door. "I have

21

a store online that specializes in these. I make and sell other stuff too, but these always make a big profit, usually because I can pick them up so cheap."

I shove the box across the backseat to my side.

"What do you make out of them?" he asks when I reemerge to grab the other box.

"All kinds of stuff. Pretty much anything creepy. I'll usually paint them to look dead or like zombies. Sometimes I'll use them as a base to make baby versions of popular horror icons, like Michael or Jason or Freddy."

"That is…" I wait for him to make the same face a lot of people do. "Well, it's pretty fucking awesome."

"Yeah?"

"Hell yeah. I love old-school horror films like that. They don't make them like they used to, that's for sure."

"Right? They aren't even scary anymore, just rely on jump scares you can see coming from a mile away."

I grunt when I grab the second box so he can drop his stuff into the trunk. It's much heavier than the first, and I can already feel sweat beginning to form on the back of my neck. I'm sure I look real attractive right now.

"Totally not scary." He sets his three bags in the trunk, then grabs the box of doll parts from my hands. I want to protest, but something tells me he wouldn't let me carry it anyway. "Did you see the one with the ghost hunters?"

"The ones who turned out to be dead the whole time?"

"Yeah."

He rolls his eyes, then disappears into the backseat momentarily. When he reappears, he places his arms on the hood of the car and runs his hand over the stubble that's lining his sharp jaw. Shit, when did that move become hot?

"What about the one with the family who moved into the farmhouse and they ended up being stalked by the farmhand who showed up literally every time something creepy happened and they never put two and two together?"

"That one had me raging at the screen. Like, come on! First, why do you move into a house where a double murder happened and then act all surprised when spooky stuff starts taking place? Second, he was literally there every time! It was obviously him!"

He chuckles. "So awful."

We grow quiet, the faint sounds of insects beginning to come to life in the nearby forest.

Even though we're not speaking, I don't feel like I need to fill the silence. It's weird how easy it is to talk to him, but I'm also thankful because we have a solid four hours ahead of us.

"So, uh, is that everything you need from your car?"

He nods instead of answering, then reaches his hand across the hood.

"What?"

"Keys."

"What? No way."

"Yes way," he says as he pushes off the car and comes around to my side. He doesn't stop until he's right in front of me, and I have to tip my head back to look at his face. "I saw the way you were squinting just driving to my car. You're blind as fuck. You almost hit me when there was still light outside. We're about half an hour from there being none at all, and I'd really like to get to where I'm going in one piece."

I grit my teeth because he's not wrong.

I am blind as fuck at night. It's why I was so annoyed when my mom insisted we go for lunch with my sister this afternoon. It ran long just like I knew it would and put me a good two hours behind when I wanted to leave to avoid driving at night.

"You can trust me, Harper."

I stare up at him, and my mouth goes dry.

Can I trust him?

I don't know why I'm hesitating all of a sudden, why just now my nerves are on edge.

Maybe it's the reality that I'm about to drive multiple hours with someone I don't know sitting beside me. Someone insanely attractive on top of it.

Or maybe it's that handing him my keys is like handing over my life to him.

I drop them into his outstretched hand. "If you wreck my car, I swear, I'll—"

"Shoot me with your gun?"

"Yes!"

That part I didn't lie about. I do have a gun.

"Right," he says, not looking the least bit threatened. "Duly noted. Let's get on the road, then."

I march over to the passenger side and climb into my car. It feels weird being on this side of the vehicle, and not just because I have to pull the seat way up.

The car isn't much to most people, but it's mine and it's completely paid for, which is a big bonus in my eyes. I wanted something reliable, and this has proved to be just that.

Granted, I didn't think it was that small when I bought it, but I know it just feels that way now because of Collin taking up most of the room.

I watch the way his muscles jump as he navigates us back onto the road. He looks calm and collected—and a lot more confident driving than I did as night falls around us.

Several miles pass before either of us speaks.

"Do you do it full-time?"

My brows pinch together at his question, and he peeks over at me when I don't answer right away.

"The dolls," he clarifies. "Is that what you do full-time?"

I nod. "It is. I went to school for art and found I had a knack for creating props and such."

"Wouldn't that be a job more suited for California? Hollywood and such?"

"Ever heard of the internet?" I cringe at the sarcasm

that drips from my words. "Sorry. I'm not exactly good with people, and sometimes my words come out a little harsher than I intend."

"I mean, my first impression of you was you trying to run me over. Little hard to top that at this point."

Another cringe. "Sorry."

He laughs. "All good. You're more than making up for it by giving me a ride. My co—boss would probably have my ass for getting in a car with someone I don't know, but I bet he'd be even more pissed if I was roadkill."

"I doubt you would have died. I wasn't even going that fast."

He gives me a look that clearly says I'm full of shit before returning his gaze to the road.

"Fine." I huff. "So you'd maybe be a little dead. I'm really glad I didn't kill you though. That would have looked so bad for my business."

"Yes, your business being in jeopardy was my biggest concern too."

A smile tugs at his lips.

Maybe my surprise road trip buddy won't be so bad after all.

CHAPTER 3

"You take that back right now, mister!"

I shake my head. "No way. I'm right and you know it."

"You are wrong. So unbelievably wrong. Michael is a million times better than Freddy."

"Is he, though? Freddy is hilarious and scary—that perfect combination."

"Is he, though?" she tosses back. "Michael is menacing. He's just always...there. Watching and waiting." She lets out a shiver. "It's creepy."

"It's predictable. Stalk, stab, chase, repeat." I roll my eyes. "Freddy is the complete opposite. You never know what the hell the dude is going to do next."

"Except call you a bitch. He always calls his victims a bitch. *I'm coming for you, bitch*," she mocks in a deep voice. "Oh god, those movies are so cheesy."

"Absolutely awful. But somehow still addicting and good? Except for that reboot. That was terrible."

"Oddly enough, I thought it was too dark."

"Agreed. They tried taking it way too seriously."

"What about *Freddy vs. Jason?*"

"Absolute classic. A masterpiece."

"Kia, he has asthma!" she quotes, and we fall into laughter again.

A loud rumble echoes over our sounds.

Now it's just Harper who is laughing as I cringe.

"Was that your stomach?" I nod. "Hungry?"

"Fucking starved. I usually have a pretty set schedule for meals, and I'm about four hours past that right now."

"You could have said something or just taken us through a drive-thru."

I could have, but it didn't feel right whipping into a fast-food joint. She's already doing me a favor by giving me a ride. I don't want to add more time to her journey.

"Pull off at the next exit," she instructs, pointing at the sign as we pass it. "I could go for something to eat myself. You don't mind eating while driving, do you?"

"I think I can manage."

We've been on the road for an hour now, but we've only made it another thirty miles after hitting a long stretch of construction where we had to sit in traffic for half an hour. Thanks to that, we're somehow still at least a few hours away from our destination.

I stifle a yawn, already knowing I'm going to be bone-tired for practice tomorrow.

I hit the next exit and we slowly make our way through the town, looking for something to eat. It's fairly barren with only one drive-thru open.

"Well, guess that eliminates the whole 'where do you want to eat' conversation that always ends in an argument," she says as I pull into the short line.

"If you weren't going to pick a place, I'd have just gone wherever I wanted to eat and you'd either find something or you wouldn't."

Her brows shoot up in a way that says *Seriously?*

I shrug. "I don't play around when it comes to food."

"Noted."

I place our order: two cheeseburgers and chicken nuggets for me and a burger with fries for her.

"Here." I look over to find Harper holding her debit card my way.

I return her lifted-brow stare from earlier. "Not happening."

She shoves it my way again, and I shake my head. She gives up with a groan, slipping it back into her wallet before tucking it into her purse. "You're kind of annoying."

I chuckle. "I'll take into serious consideration from now on that the girl who tried to run me over finds me annoying."

She crosses her arms with a huff. "Are you going to hold that against me forever?"

"Oh, I'm sorry, am I supposed to forget about it already?"

"It's been over an hour."

"Right." I smack my forehead. "I forgot that all

traumatic events only have an hour-long window for when I'm allowed to be salty about them."

"Wow. So you're not just annoying, you're also dramatic."

"I thought I was only *kind of* annoying."

"You've leveled up. Congratulations."

But there's a smile on her face when she says it.

Even under the harsh yellow lights of the drive-thru, she's still cute with her arms crossed and eyes narrowed, lips pinched tightly together.

She told me the reason she's driving from Howardsville to Bartlett is because her older sister is getting married and she had to go home for an engagement party. I've never understood the point of those, but she seemed excited about it, so I didn't say anything to crush her spirit.

When she asked me what I do, I quickly shifted the conversation back to her. She lit up like the sky on a July night and animatedly began talking about her love of all things horror. We started comparing our favorites, and the conversation has flowed naturally...and away from me. Just how I like it.

Talking with her has been so easy that I haven't once thought about losing the Cup. Or the fact that my teammates probably hate me and I have to face them tomorrow.

I wince. *Never mind. There it is.*

Harper busies herself with her phone, and it takes a lot for me to not peek at the screen to see what she's doing.

It's a dick move, but I want to know if she's recognized me yet, if she's plugging my name into Google just to see all the shitty things I've done lately.

We pull up to the window to pay, and the moment the kid behind the register sees me, recognition dawns on his face. His eyes go wide and his mouth drops open.

Please don't say anything. Please don't say anything.

"Shit," the kid mumbles. "You... You're Col—"

"One sweet tea and one unsweet," I interrupt, turning my body to block his reaction from Harper's view. I don't want this to turn into a big deal and have her asking too many questions. While she still hasn't indicated she has a clue who I am, I don't want to risk a scene. "Kind of in a hurry."

"Right. Of course. Totally get it. But do you mind..." The kid, who doesn't seem old enough to be out of high school, holds a pen my way.

"Sure. No problem." I grab it and scribble my name on the blank receipt paper he hands over to me.

"Thanks, man. I'm a big fan."

"Love to hear it." I shoot him a grin. "Can I get those drinks?"

"Oh, shit. Right. Be right back."

The kid scurries off, and I relax back into the seat.

I'm used to getting noticed, but a lot of times the people around town let me be. Sure, they'll gawk at me and sometimes ask for an autograph, but I think with seeing me every day and realizing I'm just a normal person, the fame has kind of worn off for them. Something I'm undoubtedly grateful for.

Some players enter the NHL with dreams of fame and fortune and having their faces splashed everywhere. And some enter because they're married to the game and all they're jonesing for is their next shift on the ice.

I fall into the latter category.

Fortune? Well, you don't see me bitching about being paid to play the game I love.

Fame? I'd rather take a puck to the gut from Zdeno Chara than be forced into the limelight.

It's why I've always kept a low profile. My private life is just that—private. I don't do big parties and I don't get caught with my pants down. I keep my head down and I play the game. I don't do relationships and I don't really let people into my circle.

Until recently, I've kind of been known for being tightlipped about things. Now that all my history has been broadcast for the world to see, I'm having a harder time keeping to myself.

The kid returns to the window with our drinks and food, and I try to hand him my card again but he shakes his head.

"No way. It's on me."

Normally I'd argue, but right now I just want to get my food and go before more people start to recognize me. I can already see a few employees in the background trying to take sneaky looks.

"Thanks. Appreciate it."

I grab the food and give the kid another wave before hitting the gas just a little too hard in an effort to get out of there quickly.

"What was that all about?" Harper asks, taking the bag from my lap. "You took off like a bat out of hell."

"Just not used to the car, is all," I explain.

"Fair enough. Since we've stopped, we should probably pop over to that gas station too. Top off the tank just in case we hit any more of that construction traffic."

Shit. Probably not a bad idea.

I pull into the gas station right across the street.

"Can you pump? I better go pee before we get back on the road."

"Sure."

She shoves that damn debit card at me again. "Here. Use this."

"Harper..." I groan.

"Just shut up and use it, dammit. You don't know me very well, Collin, but I'm stubborn as shit. So you'd better use it or I swear I'll make a scene."

There's a glint in her eye that tells me she isn't lying.

"Fine," I tell her, though I have no intentions of actually using her card. "Hurry up though. No dawdling or I'm sending Freddy in after you."

"Oooh, I'm shaking in my boots at the thought." She lifts her eyes skyward, then darts from the car, dashing into the small gas station.

I slide my card into the pump—she'll never even

know the difference—and stick the nozzle into the car, then lean against it, hoping she doesn't take too long inside.

A car pulls up at the pump next to me, and I pull my hat down low.

It's pointless though. As soon as the driver steps out, I see the familiar look of shock.

I give the guy a tight smile and look anywhere but at him. He takes the hint as he slides his card into the pump, then starts filling up his tank.

Except with my luck, it doesn't stick.

"You're Collin Wright, yeah?" He gives me a sad smile I'm beginning to recognize from fans. "Tough loss in Game Six, man."

You're fucking telling me.

"Yeah, wasn't my best night."

"That guy totally dove though. I can't believe they called you on that penalty. Such bullshit, bro."

It *was* bullshit. The biggest sack of it I've ever seen too.

Everyone who watched the tape back knew he dove. They knew I didn't do shit. But it doesn't matter. I had my stick there in a prone position and he took the opportunity.

I created the chance and let him take it.

I cost us the game.

"And those arrests? Man, that one…you were a minor. Shit doesn't count. And everyone knows what happened at the bar was a joke." He scoffs, shaking his head. "But don't sweat it, dude. I'm sure everyone has already forgotten about it. You're gonna kick ass this season. I can feel it."

Has everyone forgotten though? I've kept off social media for the summer, but that doesn't mean I haven't heard the rumors.

There have been countless articles wondering how I'm going to screw up and get arrested again. They already have a name coined—the Hothead Hat Trick—just waiting for the other shoe to drop.

"What'd you say your name was?"

"Max."

"Thanks, Max," I say, sticking my hand out to him.

He beams down at it with shock, then finally latches on, giving me an excited shake.

"The team is grateful for fans like you," I tell him. "We're gonna need your support this season."

"I ain't no fair-weather fan. We've gone this long without a Cup. I'm not turning my back on my team now."

Even though they're pissed at me, I'm not turning my back on them either.

My pump clicks and I tap the nozzle against the gas tank a few times. I replace it, then screw on the cap as the bell chimes.

"Oh my god, Collin!" I glance up to see Harper looking at me with big, excited eyes. "They have pickled sausages! Can you believe it? I'm grabbing some!"

She scurries back into the gas station with a new pep in her step.

I watch as she races through the aisles, then deposits two arms full of candy and snacks on the counter.

She looks…cute.

Man, I gotta stop calling her that.

But there's really no other way to describe her.

I know you shouldn't judge people based on how they look, but the fact that the girl wearing a pair of cutoff shorts, a t-shirt covered in pink flowers, and glitter Converse makes horror props? Yeah, fucking color me surprised by that.

Even though I don't really know her, I think it sort of fits. She seems to march to the beat of her own drum, and I like that.

"Hey, uh, Collin?" I turn back to the guy at the pump who is now holding a pen and a piece of paper. "Mind if I get an autograph?"

I paste on my fan smile. "I'll do you one better."

I pop the trunk of Harper's Honda and feel around my hockey bag for a puck. When I finally pluck one free, I scrawl my name across it, then hand it over to the guy.

"Here you go. As I said, the team needs more fans like you."

He stares down at it with amazement. "Holy…damn, man. Thank you. Think I could get another one? My… buddy is a big fan too."

There's something in the way he says it that reminds me of the way my brother introduces his boyfriend to people he's not so sure are willing to accept his sexuality.

I take a chance and grab one of the few Pride Night pucks I have tucked into my bag, sign it, and hand it over.

His eyes widen as he looks from the puck to me and back again.

"I brought those for my brother to give out at the safe house. Had a few extras left over."

He swallows, nodding. "I appreciate it."

"And we appreciate you, Max."

"Hey, you—oh. Sorry."

I spin around to find Harper holding two bags, which I can see are stuffed with all kinds of things, including...*is that a blanket?*

I slam the trunk closed, not wanting her to see my hockey gear that I brought with me in case I wanted to train, and turn back to Max.

"Thanks again," he says, giving me a big smile.

"Sure thing. Any time."

I turn back to Harper. "You ready?"

She nods, eyeing Max curiously as she makes her way to the passenger door.

I wait for her to get into the car before I blow out a heavy breath.

Maybe I should just tell her who I am. Let her make her own decisions about me. Maybe she won't give a shit about my status.

Or maybe she will, like everyone else does.

Maybe she'll use it against me or for her own gain like so many others have.

I don't know…it's kind of nice just being Collin Wright, an everyday guy, instead of Collin Wright, an NHL player with an impressive stats sheet and arrest record.

I wince, not wanting to think about that now.

When I finally climb back into the driver's seat, Harper's busy digging through her bags.

"Did you buy the whole store?"

She peeks up at me with guilty eyes. "Maybe? Did I mention gas stations are kind of my weakness? I always end up spending my emergency cash in them. I can't help myself."

"You didn't mention that, or else I wouldn't have let you run wild in there."

"I can't help it!" She laughs. "They always have the coolest stuff." She pulls a blanket from the bag, then wraps it around her shoulders, snuggling it close. "Plus, gas station blankets are the best."

I shake my head, grinning as I turn over the engine. "I'll take your word for it."

"You should. What did that guy want?"

"Huh?" I play dumb. "Oh, he, uh, needed some cash for gas." My stomach turns at the lie. "Did I hear you say something about pickled sausages?"

"Oh!" She dives back into the bag, searching around for her emergency pickled sausage.

Bullet dodged.

CHAPTER 4

Collin is…strange.

He doesn't scare me or worry me, and I actually feel very safe in the car with him.

But it hasn't escaped my notice that he's definitely hiding something.

I just can't put my finger on what it is.

The cashier at the gas station kept peeking over at him like he was somebody he knew. Then the guy at the gas pump kept staring at him in wonder.

At first, I figured it was nothing, like maybe he just has one of those familiar faces. But the way he keeps avoiding answering any personal questions has me suspecting otherwise.

Either way, it's really none of my business. As long as we get to our destination and he doesn't murder me, I'm calling it a win.

Besides, it's not like I'll ever see the guy again after tonight.

"Dip me," he says, holding up a chicken nugget.

We've been back on the road for an hour now, and I have no idea how he's still hungry after blazing through two cheeseburgers, half of my fries, and a pickled sausage that did not go over well with him.

"How the hell are you still eating?"

"I'm a growing boy," he answers me. "And besides, I need to get the taste of pickled sausage out of my mouth." He grimaces. "Now dip me, woman."

I roll my eyes and hold up a cup of ketchup. He dunks his nugget in it, the same thing we've been doing for the last ten minutes, and pops it into his mouth in one bite. He demands a dip, and I provide it.

"I find it completely disgusting that you're eating chicken nuggets with ketchup when there are so many other amazing sauces to be dipping them in."

He swallows his bite, and it's kind of ridiculous of me to be impressed that a guy is swallowing his food before talking. "Ketchup is the king of condiments. It's the first one we all try as children. If you think just because I'm an almost-thirty-year-old man I am not going to still have a love affair with ketchup, you're dead wrong."

So he's almost thirty, huh.

"I'm twenty-seven, by the way," he says like he can hear my thoughts. Then he grabs another chicken nugget. "Dip me."

Our arms brush as he returns his hands to the steering wheel, and I try to ignore it just like I've been trying to ignore it this whole time.

"Twenty-four," I answer his unasked question.

"Huh. A twenty-four-year-old successful woman who runs her own business. Nice."

He pops his nugget into his mouth.

"A twenty-seven-year-old from Kansas who now works in North Carolina at some mysterious corporation."

I see the muscles in his jaw jump.

Yeah, so I'm digging for information—big deal. The dude is a steel trap, and I'm curious.

"Sports industry," he says after several quiet beats.

That's the big secret? Sports?

When I don't say anything, he peeks over at me.

"I work in the sports industry."

"Are you mad because I said I don't like sports? Because I was just joking about you talking my ear off about them. I really don't care if sports are your thing. They just aren't mine."

"So you don't watch any sports? Not even with your boyfriend?"

I laugh at his completely obvious way of asking if I have a boyfriend. "No boyfriend. I am very single. Thank you for the reminder. Though you could have just outright asked me."

"Good."

I lift my brow. "Good that I don't have a boyfriend?"

Is he...interested?

"Yeah. Don't want to get you in trouble or anything."

Oh.

"If I had a boyfriend who got pissed about me

41

helping a stranger, I wouldn't want him to be my boyfriend anymore."

"To be fair, I'd be pissed as hell if my girlfriend was dumb enough to let some random weirdo into her car."

"Dumb, huh?"

"Completely."

He doesn't look the least bit sorry for saying it, and I don't entirely blame him. It was dumb. So stupid.

But Collin doesn't scare me.

My gut is telling me I can trust him, and my gut has never been wrong before.

"Well, your girlfriend doesn't have to worry about me hitting on you."

"No, she just has to worry about you trying to hit me." I groan, and he chuckles. "And you could have just outright asked me, you know." He smirks, feeling proud of throwing my words back at me. "I don't have a girlfriend."

"Good."

"Good?" he echoes.

"Yeah. Wouldn't want you to get in trouble."

Another smirk.

I ignore the way it makes my heart race a little faster.

"To answer your question, no, I don't watch any sports. I couldn't tell you a thing about them. I used to watch some with my dad, but I only did that to spend time with him." I swallow thickly, not wanting to get into the sad tale of how I used to watch games with my father, but now that he's dead, it doesn't feel the same.

He'll give me that pitying look everyone does, and I really don't want that from him. "It didn't stick though. I gave it up."

"What does he like to watch?"

"Football." His head bobs at my answer. "But don't go getting ideas about talking sports all of a sudden. I've already warned you about my penchant to fall asleep when they're discussed."

He grins. "Fine. But can I just say that experiencing live games is so different from watching it on your television?"

"I'll keep that in mind."

He looks like he wants to say something but thinks better of it.

Instead, he holds up another chicken nugget. "You gonna dip me or what?"

"Has anyone ever told you you're needy?"

"Woman…" he growls, and I laugh, giving him his precious ketchup.

When I open my eyes, we're on the bridge leading into the downtown area.

I'm not sure when it happened, but at some point during the drive, I must have rested my head against the window and passed out.

I shift in my seat, my back screaming at me for sitting in the same position for so long. My new blanket is wrapped around me, though I don't remember doing that myself.

Oh hell.

How stupid can I be for falling asleep? Anything could have happened to me. He could have driven me to his secret lair and kidnapped me forever. Or worse.

I am such an idiot.

"Hey," Collin says softly. "You're up."

I brush my hair out of my eyes, wipe at the drool that's dried on my face, and then peek over at him.

"You fell asleep," he explains.

"Gee, thanks for that astute observation."

His eyes narrow. "Someone's cranky when they wake up. And for the record, I don't have a lair."

Oh shit. I must have been talking out loud. "I'm only cranky when I wake up next to strangers who have kidnapped me in the middle of the night."

"Well, if you hadn't fallen asleep, you'd know there was a bad accident and we got rerouted. It's just after midnight."

"It added that much time to the trip?"

"That traffic was a bitch." He scrubs a hand over his jaw as he yawns. "My fucking back is killing me after all that."

"Wait—I thought you were going to Jonesville?"

He winces, peeking over at me. "I lied. I didn't want you to know where I was really going until I knew you weren't some psycho."

"Oh my god. Almost hit a guy with your car *one time* and suddenly you're some psycho."

I'm not mad. Not really. It was honestly probably a smart move and what I should have done.

I'm going to chalk all my bad decisions up to being in shock over almost ending someone's life.

"I figured I'd let you sleep so you can be rested to get to where you're going. I don't know how long your drive is, but I'm just a few blocks up here."

Does he live downtown?

That's...not cheap. At all.

He must make a killing doing whatever it is he does. His car wasn't anything flashy, but maybe it's a sentimental thing?

I shake my head. Whatever. I shouldn't be judging him right now.

Collin drives a few more blocks before expertly parallel-parking the car right in front of a building where the rent is easily twice what mine is.

He shuts the engine off, and uncomfortable silence falls over us.

It's the first time since we've been in the same car that I've felt this way. This sense of...uncertainty. The ride with him has been surprisingly easy. Natural.

But this moment?

It feels like climbing a hill with no end in sight.

After what feels like hours, Collin clears his throat, the loud sound nearly making me jump.

"Well, this is me," he says lamely.

"Right."

I push the door open, and he follows suit.

We meet at the back of the car, and I watch in silence as he pulls his bags from the trunk.

I don't know what to say to him. You're welcome? Should I apologize again?

Am I supposed to give him my number? Or ask for his?

No. That's stupid. This was just one of those once-in-a-lifetime things you keep in your back pocket for a good story at a bonfire.

Loaded down with his bags, he's standing close, and even though I've been sitting next to him for hours now, this somehow feels different.

There's a thread between us, and I can't help it when I step closer to him, as if I'm being pulled.

The streetlights illuminate him with the harshest shadows yet somehow he still looks good.

His hat is flipped backward again, and those eyes of his—a color I still can't discern—are peering down at me with hesitancy. His tongue pokes out to lick at his bottom lip.

My eyes track the movement, breath catching.

And I hold it, waiting.

Waiting.

Wanting.

I...I think I want him to kiss me.

He leans closer, and I push onto my tiptoes, ready. *Eager.*

46

A loud wail comes from just up the street, and we jump away like we've been caught doing something we shouldn't.

An ambulance screams down the road and the moment is broken.

"Uh, listen, Harper, I—"

I wave my hand, taking a step back. "Let's not suddenly make this awkward, okay?"

He laughs. "Fair enough." He sticks his hand out to me. "Thanks for not killing me."

I clasp his hand and try to ignore the warmth spreading through me. "Thank you for not kidnapping me."

"I would gladly not kidnap you any time."

I roll my eyes at his stupid joke and pull my hand away, tucking it into my pocket as that awkward silence returns.

"Well..." I say, rocking back on my heels. "I better get going before it gets any later."

"Right." He nods, then steps back, a ghost of a smile on his lips. "Night, Harper."

"Goodbye, Collin."

I don't look back at him as I climb into my car and pull back onto the street.

But somehow, I know he's watching me even as my taillights disappear from view.

CHAPTER 5

COLLIN

"For fuck's sake, Wright. Have you never skated before? You look like a newborn cow looking for a tit out there. Move it or I'll move *you*."

I don't think Coach Heller—or Coach Hell as we like to call him—has any idea what a baby cow looks like. He's been a city dweller his whole life. Farm life would kill him.

I don't respond. I just push harder. I know I'm skating like ass, but I'm tired as hell.

I waited until Harper's taillights disappeared before I walked the four blocks back to my apartment. No way was I going to take her to my actual building.

When I finally dragged my ass up to the twentieth floor, I was fucking done for. I kicked off my shoes and face-planted onto my bed. I didn't move until my alarm went off at 6 AM.

Even though I didn't move, I dreamed.

And, man, were my dreams filled with Harper.

The longer we sat in that car together, the more I

liked her. She was funny, smart, and almost painfully honest, not to mention she was insanely attractive. She doesn't have that in-your-face kind of beauty. It's the subtle kind that sneaks up on you, and damn did it sneak up on me. Every time she'd shift around in the seat and those shorts of hers would ride up higher, I'd have to talk my dick down from reacting.

I wanted to ask for her number as I stood there with my bags. Wanted to ask if I could see her again. And I really fucking wanted to kiss her.

But I was too chicken to do any of it.

Instead, I let her walk away without even knowing her last name.

And this morning I palmed my cock as I thought of her. After I came, I felt like a dick. The first thing I should have done was worry about if she got home okay, not jerk to thoughts of her. For all I know, she lied about her final destination too and had an even longer drive ahead of her.

I'm such an ass.

My defense partner skates up next to me as we run drills. "Better wipe that faraway look off your face before Coach sees it."

We've been back on the ice for all of half an hour and Rhodes and I are already falling into sync with each other. It's why no matter how badly I'm skating today, Coach's threat to move me is just that—a threat.

But to move me somewhere else…a new team…

I shake my head, not wanting to think about that.

Miller, a young rookie, slides up next to us. "Has Coach ever even been on a farm before?"

A right-winger who joined the team two years ago, he's one hell of a player with a promising career ahead of him. Everyone out on this ice right now knows he's the reason we made it as far as we did last year—thanks to that overtime goal of his—but not everyone likes it. A few of the more veteran players were not happy about him earning a first-line spot.

I chuckle. "Those were my thoughts exactly."

"Hey, you idiots better not let Heller hear you talking shit about him. He'll go full *Goon* and wipe the ice with you." Lowell, our team captain, speaks low enough so the man in question doesn't hear as he skates closer to us. "Get those legs moving, boys."

Out of all the guys on the team, these three are the ones I'm closest with since we spend the most time on the ice together. Plus, they don't hate me for what happened last year, which is always a bonus.

"Beers tonight?" Rhodes asks after Lowell and Miller skate away.

"Of course," I tell him, not forgetting our first-practice tradition.

Ice time lasts a little longer than usual and then we're off to team meetings for another two hours. Somehow, those meetings are almost as exhausting as running drills.

We go over conduct rules and nutrition and all your basic bullshit we should all already know by now. By the time we're done for the day, I'm wiped and very much looking forward to that beer.

"Wright!" Coach hollers at me just as I'm about to head out.

I've been with the Comets long enough to know that means he wants to see me in his office.

I shoulder my bag and head in there, hoping whatever this is won't take too long. I need food and a fucking nap.

"Shut the door, kid," he instructs when I walk over the threshold.

I do as he says and take a seat in the chair across from him.

Coach is an older man on the shorter side. His belly is rounded—probably from all the baked goods his wife whips up—and he's missing a big patch of hair from the back of his head.

But don't let his small stature and soft features fool you—the man is a beast on the ice.

He's a Stanley Cup champion and a hell of a scrapper. He can play with the biggest and best of them and holds his own just fine.

"Good summer?" he asks, folding his hands over his stomach.

"Mostly uneventful, thank fuck."

Aside from all the small inconvenient things that happened, I managed to come out without another arrest and my name stayed out of the headlines for a few weeks.

That's a win for me.

"Heard your car broke down yesterday and you were stranded. Get that taken care of?"

How the hell does he find these things out so quickly?

"Working on it, Coach."

"Good." He nods, eyeing me with the dark brown gaze I swear sees everything. "You good, kid?"

I know what he's asking.

He's wondering if I'm ready for this season. If I've put all the shit from last year behind me. If we're going to have a problem again. If I'm willing to do whatever it takes to make sure we get back in the Finals and we win the Cup. If I'm going to flop during a contract year and make my chances of the Comets offering me a new deal even slimmer.

I need this to be a good year for me, especially after the shitshow from last season.

He knows it as well as I do.

"I'm good, Coach."

The words sound strong and steady.

But I'm honestly not fucking good.

I skated like ass this morning. Even though Rhodes and I were good, gelling like we always do, I was off with most of the team.

Some of the guys are definitely still pissed at me for taking that penalty that cost us the game. I think deep down they know it was a shit call, but they're still determined to blame someone for the loss.

That someone just happens to be me.

Coach nods, seeming to buy my response. "All right, kid. Glad to hear."

He drops his head, focusing his stare on the stack of paperwork in front of him. I stand, taking the hint that I'm dismissed.

"Wright?" Coach calls just as I'm about to walk out the door.

I peer back at him, his attention still on his desk. "Hmm?"

"Maybe keep the distractions to a minimum this season, yeah?"

I nod, even though he's not looking at me. "Understood, Coach."

What he's saying comes through loud and clear: Keep your head down. Focus on the game.

And that's just what I plan to do.

"Did you hear Colter got a chick pregnant over the break?"

"Wait…another one?"

Rhodes bobs his head. "Yeah, man. That's two bunnies in the last year, plus the chick from a couple years ago. It was all over the papers."

I wouldn't know. I've been avoiding them.

Hell, I've been avoiding anything that gets me even remotely in trouble.

Tonight is the first time I've been in a bar in months,

and I'm making sure to keep my eyes peeled for any potential issues.

I only agreed to come because I've been gone all summer and—not that I'd admit it to him—I kind of missed Rhodes.

"Kid needs to learn to wrap his shit up or keep it in his pants."

"That's what I said!" Rhodes throws his arms up, beer sloshing around in his bottle. He draws the attention of a few women sitting down at the other end of the bar, and I see the spark in their eyes when they realize who we are. "Did he not learn his lesson the first time?"

"Or second, apparently."

"I guess that's one way to get a hat trick." Rhodes winks, and I shake my head at his lame joke. "Guess that means you're off the hook though. The media is blasting the chick's story everywhere. She's talking to anyone who will listen, selling all kinds of information on him."

"This is why I don't fuck around with women." I take a pull from my beer. "They'll ruin your career."

He shrugs, picking at the label of his. "Not all of them are so bad."

"Please tell me you aren't still hooking up with Brittney."

When he doesn't say anything, I know he is.

"Dude!" I glare at him. "We talked about this. Fucking gabbed for hours like girls at that away game." I shake my head. "You need to break it off with her. She doesn't give a shit about you. She's using you."

"Hey, man, when the heart wants what it wants…"

I give him a disappointed frown, and he just shrugs.

I think she's a money-hungry bitch looking to ride his coattails, but Rhodes doesn't see her that way.

He fell for her fast. I think he told me he was going to marry her on the second date, but Brittney wasn't on the same page. She wanted something casual. No attachments…except her hand to his wallet.

They've been doing the friends-with-benefits thing for two years now, and by that I mean Rhodes sits around waiting for her to realize she's in love with him while she continues to date every idiot out there, only to run back to him when she gets her heart broken.

For some reason I cannot comprehend, he's willing to wait for her.

A few guys on the team give him shit for it, claiming she must have some magical pussy or something, but I think the poor bastard is just seriously in love with her.

"I don't want to hear shit from you. At least I'm getting laid frequently."

"Yeah, you and all the other guys she's screwing."

"We're not…that's not what we have. I can see other women if I want to," he argues, but I can see the disappointment in his eyes.

"And I'll have you know, I'm doing just fine in the getting-laid department, thank you very much."

"Really? Because you were skating like trash this morning. Trash skating means you're not relaxed. If you were getting laid, you'd be relaxed."

"Is that how that works out?"

"Yep."

All right, fine.

He's not wrong.

I haven't been laid in a long time, and I am far from relaxed lately. Not even jerking off this morning could help fix it.

But can I really be blamed? I'm stressed about getting back in the swing of things with the team. About the season. About making sure I'm toeing the line and not fucking up like I did last year. About earning a spot so I can stay with this team I love so much.

He claps me on the back. "I know that face. It's the face of a sex-deprived man."

I shrug off his hand with a scowl. "I am not sex-deprived. I'm just…focused on my game."

At the mention of sex, Harper's face pops into my head.

I remember the way she looked at me, how her eyes slowly raked over my body. How she kept staring at me when she thought I was focused on the road. The way she looked up at me as we stood on that curb just inches apart. Her lips parted, chest rising and falling in staggered breaths.

Fuck, I should have just kissed her. Should have slid my hands into her hair and pulled her close and kissed her until we were both breathless. Then I should have taken her up to my apartment and thanked her properly for the ride.

I shift on the stool, the longing that's been dormant stirring to life again.

Rhodes gives me a smug grin at my canned response. "Just face it—you're deprived."

I roll my eyes, then signal the bartender for another —and final—beer.

He pops the top off of a local IPA and slides it in front of me…along with a napkin.

There's a feminine scrawl across it, and before he says anything, I know who it's from.

"From those two at the end," the bartender says, tossing his thumb over his shoulder. "I told them you weren't interested, but they wouldn't take no for an answer."

Slapshots has become a haven of sorts for the team. The owner is a big fan of the Comets and lets us come here all the time after games. The other patrons tend to leave us alone and let us do our thing, but every now and then there are a few people who don't understand the unwritten rule and butt into our downtime.

Like tonight.

"Thanks, Rod."

He gives me a nod before wandering off to take care of another customer.

Rhodes glances down at the women who were checking him out earlier. The minute his eyes land on them, they lean forward, pressing their tits out, grinning at us.

"Well, I found you some action."

"And wind up like Colter with two baby mamas?" I shake my head. "I'll pass."

"Three—he's up to three now. And why not? They're hot."

I shrug. "Just not into it."

"Who is she?"

"Who is who?"

Rhodes lifts his brows. "Dude, I've known you almost half my life now. Don't play stupid with me. Who is the girl? Did you meet someone this summer? Is that why you're not taking those very willing girls up on their offer?"

"If you like them so much, why don't you take them up on their offer?"

He gives me a hard stare.

I sigh, knowing he's not going to let it go. "There is no girl, Rhodes."

"If there's no girl, then walk over there."

"Not interested."

He opens his mouth to say something, but I shake my head. He snaps it closed again.

I guzzle down another drink of my beer.

"Okay, fine," Rhodes says after a minute of silence. "If you won't go talk to them, at least find someone to help with your problem." He bounces his brows up and down like I don't know what he's talking about.

"Why are you so worried about what I'm doing—or not doing—with my dick?"

"Because it affects the team, man!" He says it like it's the most obvious thing in the world. "If you're out there and you're not relaxed, you're not playing well. If you don't play well, we get fucked again and don't get the Cup...again."

I flinch at his words, even though I know it's nothing personal. Still fucking stings worse than taking a puck to the thigh.

I hold my palm up. "I have a solution right here."

He smacks my hand down. "You are an NHL all-star defenseman. You do not—under any circumstances—walk your own dog. That's like a law or something."

I laugh. "A law, huh?"

"Yep." He puffs his chest out, doubling down. "It's blasphemous when you have so many options practically knocking down your door."

"You're telling me when Brittney isn't off doing whomever it is she does"—he narrows his eyes—"you don't...*relax* yourself?"

He sighs. "First, my relationship"—I scoff at his use of the word and he throws me a murderous glare—"with Brittney isn't nearly as dramatic as you make it out to be. We're more together than we aren't."

I don't know what delusional world he's living in, but I'll allow it for now.

"But a few times when we've...broken up," he continues, "it's not like I've been celibate myself."

Now *this* is surprising.

"Who?"

He shrugs. "A few different women. It wasn't a big deal."

"Yeah, but who? How? I haven't seen you go home with anyone in...well, since long before Brittney."

"Iuseapps." He tips his drink back, not meeting my eyes.

"Dude, what?"

He huffs, setting his beer back down. "I said, I use apps."

"What the fuck for?"

Another shrug. "It's...easier. I'm not exactly the best at picking women up, you know." He points at the long scar that slashes through his lips and up his cheek. "Not many are clamoring to get with this ugly mug."

I met Rhodes the summer before he got his scar. We went to the same hockey camp in Minnesota and clicked fast. Back then, he was loud and cocky, but after he took a dirty skate to the face, leaving him with a deep scar after the reconstructive surgery he had to have, he changed. Now, he's quiet. Some might even say broody. He works harder at blending in than standing out, and I know that has to do with what happened. He thinks it's all people see.

I think his scar might have to do with why he keeps going back to Brittney. She's comfortable to him. Safe. She doesn't care about his scar.

Just his wallet size.

But that's a whole other thing.

"What do they say when you show up and it's you?"

"I don't really think about that in the moment. It's no different from going home with a bunny, I guess. I'm not there for the conversation, and they don't want one either."

I suppose it would be a lot like that. It's not like I haven't done it before, taken home a bunny I mean. I just haven't done it in a long time. When you come into the NHL, your first few years are magical when it comes to women. They all want you for the title, and most of the guys give in to that temptation—myself included.

After a while, it gets old.

But the nights alone get old too.

I'm not in the market for anything serious. I want easy, dirty fun. Something casual to help channel all my extra…frustrations.

Maybe this app thing is the perfect solution to that.

"What app do you use?"

His eyes widen, brows shooting into his dark blond hairline. A slow grin pulls at his lips. "I knew you were sex-deprived."

"It's for the team," I mumble.

Though neither of us believes me.

CHAPTER 6

"I'm telling you, Harp, you should have seen the way he was looking at me. It was like he wanted to reach over the counter and strangle me."

"Well, you did tell him his bald patch was blinding you."

"Because it was!"

I laugh, shaking my head at my best friend, Ryan.

"You know we're on FaceTime and I can see you, right?"

"Oh, I am well aware."

She's sitting outside of a coffee shop, sipping what looks like bitter black coffee and scarfing down her lunch while she's on break from the salon.

We're both artists in our own way. Her medium is makeup. Mine is…well, anything I can use to make something spooky.

I grab a zombie doll and hold it in front of the phone, and Ryan screams.

"Dammit, Harper! You know I hate those damn things!"

I laugh and set the doll aside.

"I seriously hate it when you're in your studio on the phone. It's so...creepy."

She's not entirely wrong. The walls are lined with movie posters, molds, and caster pieces, and horror-themed props are sitting everywhere. It's unsettling for anyone not into the genre.

"All right, fine. I get the hint. Just let me finish up this cut real quick and I'll take a break."

Carefully, I move my scalpel through the belly of the doll, making sure I get the lines just how I want them, then pull the stuffing out and set it aside.

I'm left with a deflated baby doll that I'm going to cover with burlap, then fill with black moss and bugs and creepy crawly things to make a baby Oogie Boogie.

When I'm satisfied with my stopping point, I grab my phone and head out of my studio to the kitchen to make some coffee.

An order set to go out tomorrow catches my eye: a Freddy Krueger doll.

I instantly think of Collin.

I was crushed when he didn't ask for my number. I wasn't about to offer mine up so I could just be the pathetic girl who sits by her phone waiting for the mysterious, sexy stranger to call.

I might not be in the greatest state sex-life-wise, but I'm not that desperate...yet.

"All right. Run it by me again—what did this guy look like?" Ryan says like she knows I'm thinking about him.

I called her the morning after I dropped Collin off and told her everything. She was not happy about me letting a strange man into my car, but that was soon forgotten when I told her how hot he is.

There hasn't been one day this week that she hasn't brought him up.

Which means there hasn't been one day this week that I haven't thought about him.

Okay, fine—so I don't have to wait for Ryan to bring him up to think about him. He's stuck in my head all on his own.

But I don't think I can be blamed.

Collin *was* hot.

Like ridiculously so.

Maybe even the hottest man I have ever seen before, and I was once twenty feet from Shemar Moore at an airport.

But I don't know anything about him, so finding him is next to impossible.

Besides, if I do happen across him, how am I going to explain that I was looking for him?

Oh, hey. Remember me? I'm that crazy chick who almost hit you with my car and then coerced you into said car, forced you to eat pickled sausages, and gave you sex eyes for hours on end? Yeah, just wanted to see what you're up to.

I highly doubt that's going to go over well.

Besides, I'm sure he's forgotten all about me by now, which is what I should do too—forget about him. The city is big. If I haven't run into him before now, I likely never will.

"No. I think you've done enough internet sleuthing to last a lifetime."

"Clearly I haven't done enough because we haven't found him yet."

Ryan is determined to track him down. In her romance-loving heart, our meeting on the highway that night and both being weirdly obsessed with horror movies was fate.

I tried to tell her that her logic isn't sound because he works in the sports industry and I hate sports, but she went and pointed out my Carolina Comets bumper sticker and how maybe that's what magically drew us together.

"Because I don't know anything about him and he wanted it that way."

Collin was evasive the whole night, careful not to give me any personal details. I know he was being cautious. He wasn't just a stranger to me; I was a stranger to him too.

But now I kind of wish I had something to go off.

"Fine. If you won't let me stalk your hot-as-hell hitchhiker so you two can fall madly in love, at least let me finally set up a profile for you on BeeMine and you can find true love there. Or at least a good dick to ride for a while. You look like you need a good dicking."

The guy sitting at the table behind Ryan coughs out a laugh, his coffee spilling across the table.

She spins around. "Eavesdrop much?"

I have to stifle my own laugh at her abrasiveness, never mind that she's in a public setting and talking loudly.

That's just who Ryan is. We met at orientation our freshman year of art school and hit it off immediately, which is funny because while we're similar in a lot of ways, we're just as opposite in others.

Where Ryan is a die-hard romantic, outgoing, and snarky, I'm reserved and quiet, preferring to sit at home and get my thrills in the form of a scary movie, not going out.

And then of course there's our difference in artistic interests.

Makeup isn't the only thing she's good at. She knows how to work a camera better than anyone I know, and she's aware of it too. It's how she's amassed over a million followers across Instagram and YouTube with her makeup tutorials and photography skills.

"Anyway," she continues, tossing her long, honey-blonde curls behind her shoulder. "As I was saying, let me set you up a profile and match you with somebody. That way when you eventually do run into Hot Hitchhiker again, you can be like, 'No, sorry, I'm taken because you're an idiot and didn't ask for my number.'" She claps her hands together excitedly. "Yes! Let's do that!"

"No. Absolutely not."

"Absolutely yes."

"Ryan…"

"Harper…" she mocks, then lifts her dark green eyes skyward. "Come on. We both know you're not as happy being single as you're pretending to be."

I push off the counter I've been leaning on and set the phone down against a flower vase.

I reach for a mug, then pluck an espresso pod from the top drawer of my coffee station.

One thing I wanted most when I finally got my own apartment was a coffee bar filled with different ways to make my favorite crutch.

I squirt two pumps of vanilla and one of lavender into my mug, pop the pod into the machine, and let it work its magic. I grab creamer from the fridge and take a whiff, the sweet cream hitting my senses, then pour a healthy dose into the frother I have and work it into a nice fluff.

"Why don't you just go to a coffee shop like a normal person?" Ryan says.

"Because coffee shops are expensive."

"Yeah, but they put love into their coffees here."

"Plenty of sass too. That barista at Cup of Joe's is always giving out death stares."

"And I give them right back."

"Ryan the Lion," I tease, using the nickname I gave her in college.

She lifts her hands and growls, then winks.

I laugh.

After my father died, my mother was protective to the point that it was suffocating me. I had to beg for over a year to get her to allow me to apply to art school just on the other side of the state. When I finally got there and experienced what it was like to not be under her thumb, I felt free for the first time in years.

So, during school, I worked my ass off to save up money, and after graduation, I stayed.

Even though it's been three years since I graduated, my mother asks me to move back weekly. But I don't regret it for a second.

I owe Ryan for that. She pulled me out of my shell, forced me to stand up for myself. And I love her dearly for it.

I grab my finished espresso, pour my foam concoction on top of it, and finish it off with a few shakes of cinnamon. I take a sip as I grab my phone and walk outside to my little patio area.

I might not live in the heart of downtown, but I'm perfectly okay with that. I have an excellent view of the city from my balcony without all the extra noise.

"As for your accusation regarding my happiness, it's not true. I'm fine with being single."

She cackles at my answer, so loud and creepy I swear it came straight from a horror movie. "I love how you think you can lie to me."

"I'm not lying."

She doesn't say anything. Just pins me with a stare that makes me shrink back.

"Stop looking at me like that."

"No. Not until you admit you're lying."

"I'm—"

"Harper Dolores Kelly!"

I groan. "Don't bring out the middle name."

"Then admit it."

"Fine!" I say a little too loudly. "Fine, I'm a little lonely at times, but it's nothing that's crushing. You happy?"

"Yes." She smiles triumphantly, then realizes what she said. "Well, no. I'm not happy you're lonely—just happy you finally admitted it." She taps her fingertips together. "Now, let me fix it."

"With a dating app?"

"Yes!"

"Come on, Ryan." I scoff. "Those things are just for hooking up. Everyone knows that."

"First, what's wrong with just hooking up? You clearly need it. And second, that's not true. Look at Charlie."

She's referring to her co-worker who met a guy on some app last year. They fell madly in love with each other and just got engaged last week. Ryan has forced me out a few times, and I've seen them together. It's sickening how cute they are.

"She was the exception."

I've never done the whole dating-app thing before. The few boyfriends I've had, I met at school or through mutual friends. I will admit that since I started working from home, it has been lonely at times, and if I ever did want to meet someone, my options would be pretty limited.

Hmm…perhaps online dating wouldn't be the worst idea ever.

"I'll come over tonight," Ryan says like she can read my mind and knows I'm considering it. "We can order some subs, watch a movie, and work on your profile together."

Her eyes are bright with excitement, and she's clearly loving her plan.

I love the part about subs and a movie.

The app part? Not so much.

Truthfully, I'm in no rush to get into anything serious. But I guess finding someone to have fun with for a bit wouldn't be so bad.

"Fine," I concede.

She claps her hands together, squealing with delight.

"But!" I interrupt her celebration. "When I say I'm done, I'm done. No arguments. Got it?"

She holds her hands up to show me she's not crossing her fingers and says, "I promise."

"I don't trust you. You're probably crossing that weird lucky toe of yours."

"Ohmygosh." She glances around, making sure nobody heard me. "You bitch! I hate you. I'll bring the wine. See you tonight. Love you. Bye."

"Wow. You're just really putting it all out there, aren't you?"

"What?" I take a sip from my wineglass. It's my third and I'm definitely feeling the effects. I'm not a big drinker, and sweet wine is about all I can handle. "I'd rather be honest about my passions upfront than spring it on him later."

"True, true. But it's so…" I narrow my eyes and she holds her hands up. "Fine. Tell him all about your freak-show obsession, then."

I type and erase…then do it again.

"There," I finally say, holding the phone up to her face. "How's this?"

We've been curled up on my couch for two hours now, a bottle of wine gone between the two of us, two sub boxes empty on the coffee table, and *The Haunting of Hill House* playing in the background for noise.

Ryan snatches my phone from my hand and reads it over, types a few things, then smiles.

"There. That's it."

I look at the screen, eyes wide.

"Ryan! You cannot put that in there!"

She shrugs. "Why not? It's true, isn't it?"

My cheeks heat, and she laughs at my discomfort like a brat.

I grab the phone and erase the swallowing part she tacked on to the end, then read it through again.

. . .

I'm an awkward, horror-loving artist. I love dogs more than people, and I don't trust anyone who doesn't drink coffee. I'm not looking for a Michael to my Laurie. AKA I want a fun time, not a long time. No creeps and no foot fetishes. No exceptions.

It's…shit.

Absolute shit.

I can't do this. I can't sign up on some dating app. I am not cut out for this.

A long, perfectly manicured finger comes into view, and before I know it, a screen is popping up saying *Congratulations! Your profile is now live.*

"Now you can't back out." Ryan grins at me smugly.

"I can just delete the profile."

"You could…but you won't because you love me."

Crap. She's right.

I toss my head back on a sigh. "Ugh. This is so not for me, Ryan. You're the outgoing, fun one. I'm the laid-back, awkward one. Online dating? It's so…"

"Perfect. It's perfect. You're behind a screen. You're able to just be yourself. And the best part is, if you don't like someone, you just stop talking to them. That's way better than trying to meet someone in real life where you have to be all polite and shit and can't just walk away." She lifts a shoulder. "I can't believe we didn't do this for you before, honestly."

"Because if I were in my right mind, I would have never agreed to this."

"But you're lonely, so you did."

There she goes using that word again.

Lonely.

Until I left Collin standing on that curb, I didn't realize just how alone I was feeling.

Talking to him was easy and fun. I didn't realize I missed that simple connection with another person until I walked away from it.

I miss laughing. I miss that jolt of electricity when arms brush together.

I miss being smiled at. Being teased. Heard.

Seen.

I'm not going to hold my breath that this online-dating thing pans out.

But maybe it wouldn't be such a bad thing if it did.

CHAPTER 7

"No fucking way."

I sit up, my blanket pooling around my waist as I stare down at my phone in disbelief.

I click on the image to bring up the profile. I read the bio, laughing at the obvious *Halloween* reference. There are only three images, but I'd know that flirty smile anywhere.

"Harper."

I say her name out loud for the first time since I watched her drive away, and it doesn't escape me how much I like saying it.

For the first time since Rhodes convinced me to sign up for this stupid app, I'm actually excited.

All of my time over the last two weeks has been spent on the ice training and playing exhibition games, so I haven't had a chance to do much other than scroll a bit. I've seen at least four profiles with the same images, one who only had pictures of her feet, and another for a woman who looked old enough to be my mother.

That was enough to keep me away for a while.

But with the regular season starting soon, I need to get my shit together and fast.

So finding Harper? The girl I haven't been able to forget? Yeah, it lights a fucking spark.

Before I can talk myself out of it, I hit MATCH, then go back to her profile, looking through the few photos again.

The first one is of her and a friend. They have their arms around one another and are smiling at the camera. It looks like they're at some sort of dressy function. Her friend is blonde and definitely hot, but that's not where my focus is. It's on the floor-length navy-blue dress that seems to fit Harper like it was made for her, showing off her curves and her tits that I know were definitely hiding on our car ride because I'd remember them otherwise. Her hair is curlier than when I met her and she's wearing a lot more makeup, but she still looks beautiful.

The second is closer to the Harper I met. She's wearing a worn Fleetwood Mac shirt that looks legit vintage, not one she just picked up at the store, and a pair of cutoff shorts similar to the ones she wore before. Those same glittery Converse are on her feet.

The third is one of her at a Halloween party. She's dressed up as a dead camper from Camp Crystal Lake, and it makes me laugh because it just seems so...her.

A notification fills my screen.

YOU HAVE BEEN MATCHED!

It goes through several screens of rules for the app—

like how we can report users for being inappropriate and unmatch at any time—before I'm finally able to send something.

I type out a few messages.

Hey. It's Collin. You know, that guy you almost hit with your car.

Straight to the point.

I know what you did this summer.

Hmm. It works with her whole horror theme, but it's also creepy as shit.

SHOW ME THEM TITTIES

I erase that last one immediately, then glare at my dick because I know it's him talking. *Take it down a notch, bud.*

The truth is, I don't know how to start this conversation with her. Which sucks because talking to her before came so easy.

Now, I don't know what to say.

I could tell her it's me, but that's going to go one of two ways.

1. She'll laugh at the weird coincidence and we'll jump back into our banter.

2. She's going to think I'm a total weirdo and that I stalked her online.

I'd really hope it's the first one, but I also don't want to take my chances.

Before I can send anything, a message from her pops up.

HorrorHarper: I'm a big fan of honesty, so here goes: I only clicked MATCH because of your taste in movies. I'm not a sports person at all. *waits to be unmatched*

I'm a big fan of honesty.

Fuck.

I can't tell her it's me.

I never told her I played hockey. If I tell her it's me, she's going to ask me about my handle. Then she's going to realize I didn't tell her the whole truth about me and she'll no doubt be pissed.

I should unmatch us. Should forget about her. Just move on.

My finger hovers over the UNMATCH button.

One second ticks by.

Then another.

Five more.

I can't do it.

Because I can't *not* talk to her.

Spending those few hours in the car with her were some of the best moments I've had in a long time.

I want to feel that again.

HockeyGuy69: You don't know what you're missing, then. Hockey is life.

HorrorHarper: A bunch of grown men ramming into each other while they chase down a slice of plastic? No, thanks.

HockeyGuy69: It's rubber, not plastic.

HockeyGuy69: And it sounds very sexual when you use the word "ramming." They're called hits for a reason, you know.

. . .

HorrorHarper: I'm not sure you can complain about sexual innuendos with the number 69 in your handle.

I feel a little immature having picked that number, but I never thought I'd find anyone that interesting on this app.

HockeyGuy69: I actually meant to type in 96, but I guess we'll call it a happy accident. Bob Ross would be proud.

HorrorHarper: Please do not tell me you actually think 69-ing is fun. It's...so much work. Completely overrated. You have to worry about not suffocating a guy AND doing your part. It's not fun at all.

HockeyGuy69: If the man you're 69-ing with doesn't want to be suffocated, you're with the wrong man.

HorrorHarper: That is...noted.

I laugh.

Yeah, this is definitely Harper.

HorrorHarper: So, Hockey Guy, got a name?

Fuck. Fuck. Shit. Fuck.
I somehow wasn't prepared for that question at all. What the fuck do I tell her?

HockeyGuy69: I do.

HorrorHarper: Well? You already know mine. Fair is fair.

HockeyGuy69: Wright.

HorrorHarper: Your name is Wright?

HockeyGuy69: Yep.

It's not a complete lie.

It's my last name.

And it's a test.

With my handle being hockey-related and my obvious reference to my jersey number, if she really isn't a hockey fan, she'll have no clue it's me.

This will also mean she wasn't lying the night I met her—she really *didn't* know me.

I swallow down the bile that rises in my throat.

She's not the liar. I am.

HorrorHarper: That's…different. I like it.

HockeyGuy69: Thanks, but I can't take any credit for it.

HockeyGuy69: What's your favorite scary movie?

HorrorHarper: No. Please. Stop. The originality is killing me.

HorrorHarper: Also, it's Halloween. I know, I know—not the most original answer. But it's a classic and it breathed life into the horror genre.

. . .

I knew that. At least Collin knew that.

But Wright didn't.

HockeyGuy69: Eh. Freddy's better.

HorrorHarper: You know, I had someone tell me that same thing recently.

Oh shit.

HorrorHarper: He was wrong too.

HockeyGuy69: *right

HockeyGuy69: So, Harper, tell me about yourself.

HorrorHarper: Well, I like long walks alone in the woods, enjoy taking showers when there's a killer on the loose, and never, ever turn down the chance to yell, "Who's there?" when I hear a strange noise in my apartment, even though I live alone.

. . .

I laugh. Smartass.

HockeyGuy69: That actually made me laugh out loud.

HorrorHarper: Thank you. I'll be here all night.

HorrorHarper: Wait—that sounded way too desperate, like I'll be sleeping with my phone next to me all night.

HorrorHarper: I mean, I WILL be sleeping with my phone next to me. It's also my alarm clock because who actually owns an alarm clock anymore? I'm not a psychologist, but I feel like that's a red flag of some sort.

HorrorHarper: I'm going to just stop talking now.

HockeyGuy69: What if I told you I have an alarm clock?

HorrorHarper: OH GOD. *dies of embarrassment*

. . .

HockeyGuy69: I'm kidding. It's definitely a red flag.

HorrorHarper: *wipes brow* Phew!

HorrorHarper: I really was kidding about being here all night though. I was just crawling into bed when I got the match notification. I should probably try to get some sleep.

HockeyGuy69: You're...in bed?

HorrorHarper: I am NOT sending you pictures of me in bed.

HockeyGuy69: I didn't ask for any.

HorrorHarper: Is this some sort of reverse psychology thing where you think that just because you're all "gentlemanly" I'll be like, "Poor dude, here's a tit pic"?

HockeyGuy69: Are you offering a tit pic?

· · ·

HorrorHarper: What?! NO!

HorrorHarper: Oh god. This is going awful.

HorrorHarper: Please feel free to unmatch me at any time now.

HockeyGuy69: Nah. I don't scare that easily.

HorrorHarper: Is that a red flag?

HockeyGuy69: You're the psychologist. You tell me.

HorrorHarper: I said I WASN'T one. I'm an artist.

HockeyGuy69: Artist? What kind?

HorrorHarper: Nope, sorry, Hockey Guy. I'm tired. You'll get answers tomorrow.

. . .

HockeyGuy69: Does this mean I get to talk to you again?

HorrorHarper: That's up to you.

HorrorHarper: Good night, Wright.

HockeyGuy69: Night, Harper.

I was destined to love hockey since the day I was born and came home from the hospital wrapped in my father's old St. Louis Blues t-shirt.

Once, when I was four, I slipped away from my parents to go to the frozen pond out on our property and glided around for the ten minutes it took them to find me.

I got my butt whooped, but my parents could see it that day too—the ice is where I belong.

So, they bought me skates and signed me up for everything I was old enough for. I was a natural. Born to be out here. Hockey became second nature to me.

The ice? It's my home. It's where I feel most comfortable. Where I find my peace.

So the fact that I'm playing like shit right now? It fucking blows.

"Come on, Wright. Get it together, man. Tape to fucking tape, not tape to the Indian Ocean."

I grimace at Coach's words. He's been on my ass every day and has every right to be. If it's not Rhodes out on the ice to catch my puck, it's not going to hit the tape.

It's official: I'm off my game, and everyone knows it.

Maybe Rhodes was onto something about the stress after all. Maybe I do need to find a way to unwind, to get my mind off last season.

Or maybe it's the fact that I couldn't sleep last night because I couldn't stop thinking about Harper.

I can't believe I found her.

Well, I didn't *find* her.

I stumbled upon her. On a dating app.

The girl I haven't been able to get out of my head has fallen back into my lap just as randomly as she did the first time.

A big, six-foot-four frame skids to a stop in front of me. "Get your head in the game. We can't have you blowing our chance at the Cup *again*."

Colter came to the team last year when we were primed to win the Cup. I think he's the saltiest of them all that I let the team down.

I grit my teeth.

Don't react. Don't react. Don't fucking react.

"Hey, Colter, get anyone else pregnant this

weekend?" Rhodes bumps into the giant hard enough to knock him off-balance. "What? Your mama not teach you to wrap your willy, silly?"

Colter glares at him, and I don't bother to try to hide my smirk.

It really shouldn't be funny that Rhodes, who is wider than me and has a good inch or two on my frame, is calling a grown-ass man *silly*, but it is.

And it pisses Colter right off.

He glares at Rhodes and gets up in his face. The two stare each other down.

"Just a friendly reminder," Rhodes says, "these hands are rated E for everyone. I don't give a shit if you're my teammate or not."

I should get in the way, try to pull them apart, but a sick part of me would love to watch Rhodes take Colter down a few notches. He's a big fucker, but Rhodes is the kind of guy you don't want to drop the gloves with. He might be the laid-back quiet one most of the time, but when you set him off, he's really off.

"Something wrong, boys?" Lowell stops in front of us, eyes bouncing between the three of us.

After several beats, Colter drops back, sneering over at Rhodes. "It's nothing, *Cap*."

"Good," Lowell says, ignoring the dig, probably used to it. "Let's get back to it, then."

Lowell waits for Colter to skate away before turning to face Rhodes and me.

"Does it make me a bad captain to say I fucking hate that kid?"

Rhodes grins. "No. Guy's a fucking cock."

"A cock?"

"Yeah," Rhodes calls over his shoulder as he skates away. "Ugly and weak."

Lowell shakes his head, watching as Rhodes intentionally skates up to Colter and steals his puck, taunting him.

"I swear, sometimes it feels like I'm trying to corral children."

"You're like two years older than us."

"I stand by what I said."

I don't challenge him. I'm sure it does feel like that sometimes, especially with some of these fools.

He steps closer, crossing his arms. "I say this with all the respect in the world: you're off your shit."

I sigh. "Fuck, you think I don't know that, man?"

"It's a contract year, yeah?"

I grit my teeth again, not needing that little reminder too, and give him a single nod.

He looks out at our teammates as they skate effortlessly across the ice. "I'm pushing for you with the team and with Coach for as long as I can, but…"

He trails off, and I know where he's going.

I need to get my shit together.

And fast.

"All right. Just wanted you to know I'm here."

"Thanks, Lowell," I say quietly.

He nods once, then skates away.

We wrap up practice, and instead of heading home, I hit the gym, trying to work out my frustrations.

Rhodes comes strolling in, picking up a few dumbbells at the station beside me.

I'm on a bench doing overhead presses. He's doing some goblet squats.

"Saw you talking to Lowell." Rhodes finally breaks the silence we've been working in.

"Yeah." I do another rep.

"You good?"

"As I can be."

Another rep.

"You know, I really think you need to—"

"Relax. I know." I drop my weights with a thud and sit up, resting my arms on my thighs. "I downloaded that app."

"Yeah?" He stops doing squats and looks at me with wide eyes. "Meet anyone yet?"

I give him a noncommittal shrug because I haven't told Rhodes about Harper yet. I don't know why. Maybe because the story just sounds too fucking crazy to believe? Maybe I want to keep her to myself for a little longer? I don't know.

"I heard Miller and Lowell talking about hitting up Slapshots tonight. We could"—his lips curl—"tag along."

I laugh. He can barely get the words out. Rhodes is as much of a homebody as I am.

"I appreciate the willingness to sacrifice a night in, but you don't need to play my wingman."

"Thank fuck," he mutters. "I hate going out."

"And that's why we get along so well."

He grunts and returns his weights to the rack. "Wanna come over and watch some tapes tonight?"

No. I want to stay home and message Harper.

"Probably should," I say instead. "But I think I'm gonna just try to get some rest."

"You should take a bath."

I don't even pretend to not be shocked by his words. "You take baths? Like candles, bubbles, the whole thing?"

"Yeah." He shrugs. "Get the right music going and it's relaxing as fuck."

"I'll, uh, take that into consideration."

"Hey, don't knock that shit until you try it. Besides, it's for the team, right?"

He lifts a brow, and I know what he's getting at.

You're on thin ice.

I try to push everything out of my mind the rest of my workout, but all my fuckups are hovering at the periphery, just vying for attention.

After an intense forty-five minutes, I bid goodbye to Rhodes and hit the showers.

Coach stops me as I'm heading to my car. He doesn't even have to say anything to me. The disappointment is clear in his eyes.

The fucked-up thing is, I'd rather have my parents disappointed in me than my coach.

"Maybe go out with a few of the guys, huh? Do some bonding outside the rink."

It's not a suggestion. Not really.

"Yes, sir."

He eyes me, maybe looking for an answer to my problem.

But first, he'd have to narrow it down.

Is it the Game Six loss that's throwing me off? Definitely has something to do with it. The arrest and digging into my past and all the attention that's sucked up my energy? Yeah, because that shit blows too. The rest of my team looking at me like I'm to blame for all their problems? Yep, that's a big fucking issue.

"You'll get the groove back, kid. Just need a little time."

But I hear it...that worry lacing his voice.

And I worry too.

Coach gives me a tightlipped smile, then claps me on the back, dismissing me.

I don't breathe again until I'm tucked safely in my car.

Instead of heading home right away, I grab lunch and head to a local park, hoping the outdoors might help clear my head a bit.

After a few hours of walking and people-watching, I stop by the garage that's fixing my Land Cruiser that finally made it here just to check on things, then I make my way home.

"Hey, Beau," I say to my seventy-something-year-old doorman when I walk into my building.

"Mr. Wright! Good evening, sir. Have a good practice today?"

I want to tell him not to call me sir, but I know it's no use. In the four years I've lived here, he's never listened to me before, and I know he's not about to start now.

"It was all right. How was your day? Meghan still giving you trouble?"

His eyes light up at the mention of his wife, who he's been with for fifty years now.

"Always, but she's my favorite kind of trouble, sir."

It's the same reply he always gives me, and just like always, it makes me grin.

If there's someone out there who doesn't believe in love, I'd say give them five minutes with Beau and they'll change their minds.

"Got you something." I reach into the paper sack I have in my hand, then give him one of the Oatmeal Creme Pies I picked up at the store down the block.

His eyes get just as excited as they did when I mentioned his wife. After a scare last year, Meghan took to making sure Beau only eats healthy foods. Gone are the snack cakes and cookies he used to bring in to work. It's all chicken and rice, something he's complained about frequently.

I've been sneaking him some goodies whenever I remember. Not often, but enough to keep him smiling.

"Just between us," I say on a wink.

"Thank you." He looks at the snack like it's his last meal. "Are you in for the night, sir?"

"I am."

"Would you like me to call the elevator for you?"

"Nah. I got it." I pat his shoulder. "Have a good night, Beau."

"Good night, sir. And thank you again."

I smile at him, then take the elevator up to the twentieth floor.

I kick off my shoes and pop open a beer as soon as I walk inside. I leave the bag on the counter and put the beers into the fridge before flopping down on the couch and turning on the TV.

A mistake.

A *big* mistake.

My mugshot fills the screen on *SportsCenter*.

"So, Jonesy, what do you think? Do you think Collin Wright is going to get a hat trick in handcuffs this year?"

The screen pans over to the cohost, and I hit the power button as soon as he opens his mouth.

Great. The season hasn't even officially started and I'm already being harassed.

I blow out a breath and down the rest of my beer, all the frustration that was just beginning to leave my body hitting me full force again.

"Fuck it," I mutter, pushing off of the couch.

I drop my empty bottle into the recycling, grab the grocery bag and another beer, and head to the bathroom.

I set my beer down on the counter, then empty my

pockets. I turn the water on and let it begin filling up the tub I've literally never used in my four years living here.

The real estate agent was super excited about it when I moved in, telling me I could use it to recuperate after games, but I've never bothered. The only kind of bath I've ever taken is an ice bath, and I do those at the rink.

While the tub fills, I grab the bottle of bubbles and Epsom salt I got from the store and dump a healthy amount of both in. I pull out the single wick lavender candle I bought and give it a light with the matches I picked up, then set it on the ledge of the tub.

When the tub is nice and full and the water is steaming, I strip, grab my beer and Oatmeal Creme Pie —totally fine to eat in the tub, right?—and climb in.

It's a little warm but not so unbearable I can't get used to it.

I set my phone to some classical music playlist and lean back, closing my eyes.

Just relax, Collin. Let it all go. You're healthy, you're still young. You have a fuckton of playing years left. Get out of your head and chill.

I try to conjure up the last time I felt relaxed, and the only thing that comes to mind is my car ride with Harper.

The way she made me laugh and kept my chicken nuggets sauced. The way she wasn't afraid to joke around and be playful. Hell, even when she fell asleep next to me and left me alone with my thoughts, I still felt at ease.

I need *that* feeling back.

I reach for my phone and pull up BeeMine, clicking back to our messages from last night. I read them over, smiling at her smartassery.

She said it was up to me if we talked again.

And I really want to talk again.

CHAPTER 8

"Just one more…"

I trap my tongue between my lips, something I'm well aware I do when I'm concentrating extra hard, and give the project at hand all of my attention.

"There!" I say to nobody at all when I complete the last stitch I've been painfully gluing on the zombie girl I've been working on for the last four hours.

I sit back to admire my work. They're gorgeous, maybe some of my best pieces yet.

It's a custom order for a customer who lives in Canada. She wanted a matching zombie king and queen for her and her fiancé who are getting married next month. They're doing a Halloween-themed wedding, and she wanted to surprise him with them.

I set them aside to sleep on before I decide if they're finished or not. It's the same thing I do with every project. I believe every artist needs to walk away from their craft and look at it with a fresh eye in the morning.

Sometimes letting it settle shines a light on the problem areas.

And sometimes it shines a light on the parts you never thought could be your favorite.

I click my work lamp off, then grab my coffee, which has long since turned cold, and shut down my studio for the night.

I don't have any plans and could keep working, but I promised myself when I started my business that I'd set office hours and stick to them.

I dump my cold coffee out, rinse the cup, and refill it with some white wine before heading to my bedroom to change into my pajamas. I swap my leggings for shorts and my paint-covered shirt for a camisole, then make my way back for my wine.

I sigh when I finally settle onto the couch with my drink and a bag of cheesy popcorn that I plan to devour while I watch more of *The Haunting of Hill House*.

Most people react to my love of horror like Ryan—confused and not into it.

But sometimes people like Collin come along and embrace it.

Collin.

I'll admit it—any time I've left my apartment over the last few weeks, I've been looking for him. It's silly, really. The chances of running into the guy are so slim it's unreal, but I can't help but let my eyes wander, seeking him out.

I thought I might have seen his face on TV the other

night when Ryan forced me out to dinner, but the channel had changed before I could do a double take.

Besides, why would Collin be on TV?

I pick up my phone while I munch on my popcorn, the Crain family saga playing in the background while I scroll through social media. Ryan insisted I set up an account for my business. At first, I resisted because I've always been wary of social media, but—much like she always does—she convinced me to give it a shot. Honestly, I'm glad I did. My sales were good before I had any accounts, but since I began posting regularly, my orders have really taken off. Now almost half of my custom orders are a result of posts I make.

My eyes slide up to a notification that comes through, then shift back to the task at hand.

Wait a minute...

I click the notification from BeeMine and my stomach does a little flip.

HockeyGuy69: So since you were honest with me about your disdain for hockey—something we'll come back to later—I have to confess something to you.

HockeyGuy69: I'm 27 years old and I've never taken a bath before (obviously not counting being a baby), and I'm currently sitting in a tub full of bubbles.

. . .

HorrorHarper: Did you light a candle?

HockeyGuy69: What is it with baths and candles?

HockeyGuy69: And yes.

HorrorHarper: Do you have relaxing music playing?

HockeyGuy69: I do.

HorrorHarper: Have alcohol present? (assuming you drink)

HockeyGuy69: I do, and yes.

HorrorHarper: And are you eating pizza?

HockeyGuy69: I have an Oatmeal Creme Pie.

HorrorHarper: Ding Dongs are better, but I'll allow it.

. . .

HockeyGuy69: *barely resists making a dong joke*

HockeyGuy69: But thank you. So glad I have your approval. I was worried you'd judge me.

HorrorHarper: For bathing? It's more than most men do.

HockeyGuy69: I'd be offended, but yeah, you're right.

HorrorHarper: Honestly, it makes me a little jealous. I wish I could be in the tub with you right now.

HorrorHarper: WAIT.

HorrorHarper: NO.

HorrorHarper: ABORT ABORT!

. . .

HorrorHarper: I meant in the tub too. Like in general. And alone. But like...still with you because we'd be messaging.

HorrorHarper: Yeah, that's totally what I meant.

HorrorHarper: Wow. This conversation is already going really well.

HorrorHarper: Scare you off yet?

HockeyGuy69: Not even close. I kind of like it when you get yourself all worked up over me.

HockeyGuy69: Oh shit. I think you're rubbing off on me.

HorrorHarper: As long as you're not rubbing off on me, we're fine.

I stare down at my phone in disbelief.

NO!

No, no, no.

What the hell is wrong with you, Harper? This *is why you can't find anyone to date. You're awkward. You say the first thing that pops into your head. Get a grip, woman!*

HockeyGuy69: Well, that took a turn.

HockeyGuy69: Now I'm really wishing I made that dong joke after all.

HorrorHarper: To be fair, you started this conversation off on the wrong foot.

HorrorHarper: Messaged me just to brag about you being naked.

HorrorHarper: I'm onto you.

HockeyGuy69: If only you were ON me instead...

HockeyGuy69: There. Now we're even.

· · ·

HorrorHarper: You did that on purpose to make me feel better.

HockeyGuy69: Did it work?

HorrorHarper: A little.

HockeyGuy69: Change of subject…

HorrorHarper: Are you supposed to warn about those? Or just glide right into it?

HockeyGuy69: *scrapes mind out of gutter*

HockeyGuy69: We're naturals at this.

HorrorHarper: Totally not awkward at all.

HockeyGuy69: Not one bit.

. . .

HockeyGuy69: So, you mentioned last night that you're an artist. What kind?

HorrorHarper: Finally! A safe subject!

HorrorHarper: My medium is YES and my specialty is horror. Shocking, I know.

HockeyGuy69: Medium?

HorrorHarper: Yeah, what I use to create my art. Like for a painter, their medium is what they paint on or what types of paint they use. A sculptor would be stone or clay. Mine is a little bit of everything.

HorrorHarper: I make a lot of props, sometimes for low-budget movies or displays for haunted houses. I sell stuff online and make custom orders too. And whenever I'm feeling in the mood, I paint and put those up in a local gallery that sells creations from artists in the area.

HockeyGuy69: Wow. You do all that? I feel kind of lazy now.

. . .

HockeyGuy69: *sips beer in bathtub*

HorrorHarper: It's really nothing that impressive.

HockeyGuy69: Somehow, I doubt that.

HorrorHarper: What about you? Any artistic abilities?

HockeyGuy69: Not really.

HorrorHarper: What do you do for a living?

HockeyGuy69: Sports industry.

A sense of déjà vu hits me.

Sports industry? Where have I heard that response before?

HockeyGuy69: Sorry. I know you're not a sports fan. I won't bore you with the details.

. . .

HorrorHarper: Well, it's not really fair that I get to talk about my hobbies and you can't talk about yours.

HockeyGuy69: It's fine. I'd rather find out more about you anyway. Did you always want to be an artist?

HorrorHarper: No. I used to want to be a country singer. Then I realized I couldn't sing for shit.

HockeyGuy69: I'm sure it's not THAT bad.

HorrorHarper: When I was a kid, my parents took my sister and me to this local bar that did family karaoke on Sunday nights. I literally got booed off the stage.

HorrorHarper: I was 12.

HockeyGuy69: They booed a 12-year-old off stage?!

. . .

HorrorHarper: Someone even threw a sugar packet at me.

HorrorHarper: Either they really hated "Tim McGraw" or I was that bad.

HockeyGuy69: That sounds traumatizing.

HorrorHarper: I swear I still have stage fright because of it.

HorrorHarper: My parents also paid me to not audition for American Idol because they didn't want to be embarrassed when they inevitably played my awful audition on TV.

HockeyGuy69: That's oddly sweet of them.

HockeyGuy69: I was Peter Pan in my middle school play and farted when I was lifted by the harness to fly.

HockeyGuy69: IN A SILENT AUDITORIUM!

. . .

HockeyGuy69: They called me Peter Fartknocker until tenth grade.

HorrorHarper: 10th grade?! That's a commitment.

HockeyGuy69: Yeah, I finally hit my growth spurt and had like four inches and twenty pounds on everyone. They shut up after that.

HorrorHarper: How tall are you?

HockeyGuy69: 6'3"

I rub my thighs together.

I've always had a thing for tall men.

Not that it's shocking. I'm only five foot four. Practically everyone is taller than me.

HockeyGuy69: You know what they say about tall hockey players, right?

. . .

HorrorHarper: I'm honestly not sure if it'll be worse for you to say big dicks, socks, or shoes.

HockeyGuy69: Big sticks.

HorrorHarper: Hockey joke? That's the worst one for sure.

HockeyGuy69: I'm just glad you picked up on it. Maybe you don't hate hockey as much as you claim.

HorrorHarper: No comment.

HockeyGuy69: I'll woo you over to the dark side soon enough.

HorrorHarper: Is that what you're trying to do? Woo me, Peter Fartknocker?

HockeyGuy69: *narrows eyes* Well, not anymore, Miss Not American Idol. I got a bucket and a perfectly good tune to put in it, unlike some people.

. . .

HorrorHarper: Ouch. That one kind of stung.

HockeyGuy69: Something tells me you can take it.

HockeyGuy69: Please don't take this the wrong way, but I'm falling asleep.

HorrorHarper: Oh, yeah, totally not offended AT ALL.

HorrorHarper: *is totally offended*

HockeyGuy69: The bath kicked my ass. How do women take those all the time?

HorrorHarper: In our defense, we're always exhausted because we have to deal with men. We're used to it.

HockeyGuy69: Ouch. That one kind of stung.

. . .

I laugh at his repetition of my words.

HockeyGuy69: Can I talk to you again?

I smile down at my phone, loving how that's twice now he's asked that. Most guys wouldn't. They'd just message asking what I'm wearing or use no pretenses and send a dick pic instead.

It's…thoughtful that he asks.

HorrorHarper: That's up to you.

HockeyGuy69: Then that's a yes.

HockeyGuy69: Night, Harper.

HorrorHarper: Night, Hockey Guy.

HockeyGuy69: If you could travel anywhere in the world right now, where would you go?

• • •

I grin as I read the message from Wright, coming in right on time.

I've just curled up on the couch after declining an invitation to go out with Ryan and her friend from the salon. I know I'll have to make it up to her later, but I've been so busy trying to get these custom orders done on time and keep putting it off.

HorrorHarper: To Scotland.

HockeyGuy69: Why?

HorrorHarper: Do you even have to ask? The accents, duh!

HorrorHarper: Also so I could bring home a hot Scot and my mom would finally get off my butt about finding love or whatever.

HockeyGuy69: Oof. Guess I'm out of the running, then. No accent here.

. . .

HorrorHarper: That's too bad. I was kind of hoping you were an expat from Scotland. Or maybe even Australia.

HockeyGuy69: *don't make a down under joke, don't make a down under joke*

HorrorHarper: I'd almost be disappointed if you didn't at least think of one.

HockeyGuy69: Because you'd expect nothing less from a guy with 69 in his handle?

HorrorHarper: Yes.

HockeyGuy69: You miss a hundred percent of the shots you don't take.

HorrorHarper: Okay, Gretzky.

HockeyGuy69: Thought you weren't a hockey fan.

. . .

HorrorHarper: Don't get too excited. Everyone knows that quote. Just like everyone knows it was really Michael Scott who said it.

HockeyGuy69: *adds The Office fan to list of things I dig about you*

HorrorHarper: I want to hear more about this list…

HockeyGuy69: Nah. Haven't earned it yet.

HorrorHarper: Boo. You suck.

HorrorHarper: What about you? Where would you go for vacation?

HockeyGuy69: Gonna sound lame, but I'd go back home. Not permanently or anything, but just for a breather. I visited recently and realized how much I miss such a slow-paced life and my family, especially my brother.

. . .

HorrorHarper: It's not lame. It's actually kind of sweet.

HorrorHarper: Are you and your brother close?

HockeyGuy69: Very. We're less than two years apart and we've always been tight.

HockeyGuy69: Do you have any siblings?

HorrorHarper: One sister. She's older by two years and a huge pain in my ass sometimes. She just recently got engaged and my mom is over the moon about it and won't stop asking when it's my turn next.

HockeyGuy69: I'd propose to help you out, but I just don't think we're there yet. Maybe next week.

HorrorHarper: Next week, huh? So sure we'll still be talking then?

HockeyGuy69: I thought it was up to me.

. . .

HorrorHarper: Huh. I did say that, didn't I?

HockeyGuy69: You did.

HockeyGuy69: And since it's up to me, yes, we'll still be talking then.

HockeyGuy69: Night, Harper.

HorrorHarper: Good night, Wright.

CHAPTER 9

COLLIN

We lost four of our exhibition games. Sure, they aren't anything to truly sweat over, but it still sucks.

But that's not what has me wanting to toss my dinner back up.

What's killing me is that I know I'm playing like shit and I can't seem to get my act together. With the regular season starting in just two days—and starting on the road no less—it's beginning to worry me more and more.

Am I done? Washed up? Is hockey…*over* for me?

"So, is this something we need to be worrying about?"

I glance across the table at my agent. His water cup is held loosely in one hand, arm slung across the chair next to him. His leg is pulled up, resting on his knee as he regards me carefully.

To most, he'd appear calm, nonchalant even.

But not to me.

I see the trepidation in his eyes, and I'm sure it matches my own.

More than anything, I want to answer his question with a resounding *no*. Want to reassure him that it's nothing. That I'm just still shaking off the bad vibes of last season and I'll be ready when the season officially starts.

But I know he'll see right fucking through me.

So I don't say anything at all.

He nods, then sits forward, arms resting on the table we've been sitting at for the last hour, idly chitchatting, avoiding the real nitty-gritty of things until our stomachs were full. "All right. Let's tackle this together, then. What's going on?"

So, I tell him.

I tell him all about how I've been carrying around this dark cloud of uncertainty since the end of last season. All the bad shit that's happened. All the pressure of it being a contract year. The way my teammates are looking at me. I leave out Harper and how guilty I feel for lying to her.

When I'm finished, he doesn't speak for a long time, just watches me with those perceptive eyes.

Then he laughs.

He fucking *laughs*.

"You'll have to excuse me if I don't find this funny."

I glower at him and shove a fry into my mouth, annoyed by his reaction.

He doesn't care. He just keeps laughing.

He's lucky he's an amazing agent and has become a good friend over the years.

When Shepard Clark knocked on my door, asking if I was represented, I told him to fuck off. What the hell does a former pro-baseball star and World Series champion want with a hockey player? Turned out, a lot.

He was honest from the get-go. He and his best friend started an agency, and he wanted to step outside his comfort zone and push himself by getting immersed in another world.

There was no bullshit with him. No trying to schmooze me. Straight and to the point.

I liked him right away and signed a contract without hesitation.

Lucky for me, trusting my gut was the right thing to do. When I got arrested and the news about my prior charge came out, he didn't even bat an eye. He was just there, ready to help make it right. We've had a good, solid relationship through the years.

But right now I kind of want to punch him.

"Sorry, sorry," he finally says, then he clears his throat and shakes his shoulders, taking a drink of the water sitting in front of him. "I'm good."

"What's so fucking funny?"

"You!" He chuckles again, runs a hand through his hair. "Can't you see that it's you?" He reaches over and flicks my temple. I swat at his hand. "You're up there, not in the game like you need to be. You need to just relax. Get laid. Get a massage. Meditate."

"Not you too." I groan, tossing my head back. "Fucking Rhodes keeps saying the same shit."

"And he's right." He shrugs. "I've been in your position before, pissed at the world because it's fucking you over. But athlete to athlete, if you're not relaxed, you're not going to play well. It really is that simple."

"Tell that to my brain. It won't shut off."

"When's the last time it did? The last time you weren't completely stressed to the max? The last time you let go and had fun?"

My mind drifts to Harper and that car ride we shared.

To Harper and our texts at night.

Talking to her is easy. Effortless. Every time a conversation between us ends, I can't wait for another to begin.

"Oh." Shep draws my attention his way. "Whatever —or *whoever*—it is you're thinking about, do that...*them*. Your whole"—he waves a hand over me—"everything just changed." I scowl and he laughs, setting his water down and flagging down our server. "Listen, Col, you know I want this season to go well as much as you do. You deserve to hoist that Cup as much as any other player."

The server appears with our check in hand, and Shep slips them a black card without even looking at the bill. He can afford it. I know what he makes in commission from me alone, not to mention his other clients.

"But if you don't get out of your own way, it's not going to happen," he finishes once the server disappears again.

I let out a long sigh because somewhere deep down, I know he's probably right.

This means Rhodes is right too—not that I'd tell the asshole.

But it's not as easy as they make it sound.

Every time I'm out on the ice—the place that was once my haven—all I see are the disappointed faces of my teammates. All I hear is the deafening silence of when the call that sealed our fate was made.

Usually when you think hockey arena, you think boisterous, cheering fans.

But most people forget about the quiet moments. The ones where everyone collectively holds their breaths.

The ones where the game of inches and seconds really becomes a game of centimeters and milliseconds.

I remember them.

I remember them all too well.

"The Comets love you," he says like he can read my thoughts. "The fans love you. Your coaches, the staff, teammates—they all want to see you stay here as much as you want to stay. But…"

My gut sinks, already knowing where this is going.

"If you don't step aside and let your hockey sense take over, given your…history…we should probably start talking about the real possibility of playing somewhere else next year."

His words fall around us like a heavy curtain.

I want to stay with the Comets. As much as I love my parents and miss them, this is home now. I know there are no guarantees in hockey, but if I had a chance to work hard and make it happen, I'd stay.

The server drops off the tab, and Shep signs the receipt, then snaps the book closed with finality.

"I was hoping to stay and chat some more, but I gotta get back to the wife."

His wife, Denver, is a journalist and always keeps her ear to the ground about anything ready to blow up concerning Shep's athletes. I knew the press had dug into my past before they even aired the story thanks to her.

"Never have kids, man," he says, standing. I follow his lead, gulping down the rest of my water, then grabbing my discarded ball cap and pulling it low over my head. I'm sure most people won't bother me in the restaurant, but I still like to keep a low profile on the streets. "I swear they never stop shitting."

I laugh. "Trust me, much to my parents' dismay, I'm good on kids."

"That's what my brother said too, and I guess he was right to an extent, but those fucking goats of his are just as bad as having human children."

He shakes his head as we make our way out of the restaurant.

I only get stopped once, which is a win for me.

"Look," Shep says when we get outside, "just think about what I—" He shakes his head. "You know what? No. *Don't* think. No thinking for a change, just *doing*. Whatever feels good, do that."

I nod.

"Good. Now go home and get some rest." He claps me on the shoulder. "I'll text you, okay?"

Another nod.

He spins on his heel, then turns right back around, snapping his fingers.

"Shit, I almost forgot. Home opener? Your parents coming?"

"Nah. They have some big fall festival thing to prepare for."

"Mind if I get your seats? Denver bought some photographs from a local photographer and fell in love with the gal. They won't stop gabbing with each other. Figured we could hook her and a friend up with tickets to a home game or something."

"Of course," I say. "They're all yours. I'll get it taken care of."

"Thanks. Appreciate it." Another slap to the shoulder as he backs away. "Remember, just relax."

I flip him off, and he laughs.

I head in the opposite direction, my apartment only a couple of blocks away. I keep my head down as I make my way home, not wanting to be bothered by anyone. At the beginning of my career, this always made me feel like an asshole. I thought I had to be "on" for my fans at all times. But the more I settle into the limelight, the better I am at creating boundaries.

"Good evening, sir," Beau says, holding the door open for me as I approach. "You look like you're deep in concentration. Anything I can do to help?"

"Apparently I think too much. Think you can perform a lobotomy?"

"I once landed a plane in the water and survived floating in the ocean for five days. I was a pilot, not a doctor, but I can give it my best shot." He leans in close. "For an Oatmeal Creme Pie, sir."

I tuck my lips together at his answer. "I'm fresh out tonight. Rain check on the pie and lobotomy?"

"You bet." He sends me a wink as I step into the elevator. "Have a good night, sir."

"Good night, Beau. Say hi to Meghan for me."

Once inside my apartment, I change into a pair of sweats, forgoing a shirt, then grab a beer and settle onto the couch.

I'm physically tired, but my brain is nowhere near ready for bed. I know if I lie down now, I'll just wait for hours with no sleep in sight.

When I turn on the TV, *SportsCenter* is pulled up and I click away fast. I don't want to think about hockey tonight. I just want to watch something mindless and not think.

I settle on a rerun of *FRIENDS* and grab my phone, scrolling the internet with no real purpose.

Shep's words play in my mind over and over again.

Whatever feels good, do that.

No thinking, just doing.

I don't let myself overthink it as I navigate to the BeeMine app and click on Harper's messages.

. . .

HockeyGuy69: So…

Dots dance on my screen almost instantly, and I grin.

HorrorHarper: Oh no. Nothing good ever starts with so.

HorrorHarper: You're breaking up with me, aren't you?

HockeyGuy69: Did I miss a step in our relationship?

HorrorHarper: Well, I don't mean BREAKING UP breaking up. I mean like…you're gonna break the news that you've met someone else and you're all in love and shit and we have to stop messaging.

HorrorHarper: But because you're a total gentleman, you're telling me.

HorrorHarper: At least I have you built up in my head as a gentleman.

. . .

HorrorHarper: Are you a gentleman?

HockeyGuy69: Depends on the setting.

HorrorHarper: Oh. OH. *blushes*

HockeyGuy69: Also, I'm not messaging anyone else. Just so we're clear.

HorrorHarper: Neither am I.

HockeyGuy69: Good. That's good.

HockeyGuy69: This is a good so, by the way. I think.

HorrorHarper: You sound totally confident about that.

HockeyGuy69: What can I say? I'm a confident guy.

. . .

HorrorHarper: *waits for bombshell*

HockeyGuy69: Go out with me.

CHAPTER 10

HockeyGuy69: Go out with me.

I throw my phone.

Like clean across the room, just give it a toss.

Because what. The. Fuck?!

My phone buzzes over where it landed, and I'm scared to pick it up.

This must be what people mean when they say their heart leaped into their throat.

Because that's where mine is right now.

A...date?

Not that I haven't considered the possibility before. I mean, that's what this whole thing is supposed to be leading to, right?

All of a sudden it just feels so real. Tangible.

Exciting.

Because I think I'd like a date with Wright.

I want to know if he's this funny and bold in real life. If he's this charming.

I scramble across the room at the thought of seeing him all dressed up and pluck my phone from the floor.

HockeyGuy69: Shit. I freaked you out, didn't I?

HorrorHarper: No.

HorrorHarper: Okay, fine. Maybe.

HockeyGuy69: I guess what I should have asked was… Are you free next Saturday?

HorrorHarper: I'm always free on Saturdays.

HorrorHarper: Oh god. That makes it sound like I have no life. I swear I have a wife.

HorrorHarper: Crap! I meant LIFE.

. . .

HorrorHarper: I have a LIFE. Not a wife. Though if Kate Beckinsale came knocking at my door, I'm not entirely sure I'd turn her down.

HockeyGuy69: No sane person would.

HockeyGuy69: Also, your panicked texting is so cute.

HorrorHarper: Ah. The dreaded "cute" word.

HockeyGuy69: Is it a bad thing to be cute?

HorrorHarper: Not entirely. It's just… Well, cute always seems to be delegated to the best friend's tagalong little sister. Or the friend who makes you laugh but doesn't make you…you know…hard.

HorrorHarper: Like your penis. I'm talking about your penis getting hard.

HockeyGuy69: Harper?

. . .

HockeyGuy69: I mean this with absolutely all the respect in the world, but shut up.

HockeyGuy69: Women overthink shit way too much.

HockeyGuy69: Your rambling is cute because it means you actually care about what I think of you. You're cute because you're funny and quick-witted. Cute because you're unapologetically into what you're into. Cute because you're brave enough to put yourself out there for online dating.

HockeyGuy69: But, Harper? You're also fucking gorgeous, and I'd be damn lucky if you said yes to going on a date with me.

I read his messages over and over again with shaking hands and heated cheeks.

I feel so silly getting flustered over the word cute, but when he spells it all out like that…

HockeyGuy69: Did I scare you away?

. . .

HorrorHarper: No.

HockeyGuy69: No I didn't scare you or no to a date.

HorrorHarper: I'm not scared. Well, maybe a little. But I'm only scared because I really want to say YES to next Saturday but…I'm also worried.

HockeyGuy69: What's to worry about?

HorrorHarper: Well, you could totally murder me for starters. I'm a horror movie lover. I am well versed in the dangers of meeting strangers.

HockeyGuy69: I promise not to murder you.

HorrorHarper: Promise promise?

HockeyGuy69: Yes. I look really good in a suit as long as it's not a jumpsuit.

. . .

HorrorHarper: Why did I just get visions of you looking all hot in a Michael Myers jumpsuit?

HockeyGuy69: Because you're demented.

HockeyGuy69: Speaking of Michael...I thought your profile specifically stated you were no Laurie Strode looking for her Michael. A good time, not a long time.

HorrorHarper: True...

HockeyGuy69: Then come have a good time with me, Harper.

A date with Hockey Guy?

It's a bad idea. I just know it is.

I'm almost certain I'll be stood up or let down. That's usually how this whole internet-dating thing goes.

But I can't stop myself from letting those thoughts of *maybe* creep in.

Maybe it won't be bad.

Maybe he'll be everything I hope he is.

Maybe even more.

Before I can talk myself out of it, I respond.

HorrorHarper: Yes.

"Okay, what the hell is going on? You've looked at your phone no less than six times in the last ten minutes. This is supposed to be *our* time, remember?"

My cheeks flush under Ryan's watchful gaze.

Of course she'd pick up on that.

I don't want to be that glued-to-the-phone type of girl, but I haven't heard from him tonight and it's way past the time when he usually texts.

Did he realize he made a mistake? Was this all a game? Is he ghosting me?

Ryan gasps, slapping at the table. "Oh my gosh. *Puh-lease* tell me you met someone on that app and you've been a really bad friend by holding out on me?"

Her eyes are bright and shiny and all kinds of excited as she wiggles her fingers.

I don't want to lie to her, but I also kind of don't want to share Hockey Guy with her just yet.

But Ryan being Ryan, she knows the truth before I can even say anything.

"You are! You're totally holding out on me! Who is he? I want to see!" She reaches for my phone, but I pull it out of the way just in time. She pushes her lip out and crosses her arms over her chest, pouting. "You suck."

"These are our private messages, you nosy brat."

"Wait a minute…" She sits forward like it hits her all at once. "Harper Dolores, have you gone out on a *date* with this person?"

"No."

She narrows her eyes. "Why does that feel like a loaded answer?"

I shrink back from her piercing dark green gaze.

Not much scares me, but Ryan?

Terrifies the crap out of me.

"Because it's missing the words 'not yet,'" I mumble, taking a sip of my frozen daiquiri to avoid looking at her, waiting for her reaction.

"You…you have a *date* and you didn't tell me?"

She sounds…hurt.

And I didn't mean to hurt her.

"Yes. But the only reason I didn't say anything is because I didn't want to jinx it. We've been talking every night, and things have been going well. He asked me out."

"Shut up. When?"

"For Saturday."

"*Saturday* Saturday? Like three days from now?" I nod, and she squeals with delight. "Oh my gosh. I'm so excited for you!"

"Me too."

It's true. Even though our texts have been brief since he asked me out, there is something low in my gut telling me I can trust him.

It's that same feeling I had when I let Collin into my car.

My mind begins to drift to the stranger again, but I don't let it get far. I shouldn't be thinking of him still, not really. He was nobody. Just a fun story to tell people. That's all.

"So we've given up on Hot Hitchhiker, then?" Ryan asks like she knows I'm thinking about him.

I lift my eyes skyward. "We were never 'on' Hot Hitchhiker. *You* were the one obsessed with him."

"Uh-huh. Says the girl who blushed the entire time she talked about him." She takes a sip of her cocktail, lifting a pointed brow my way. "Anyway, let's see our new boyfriend. Is he hot?"

I click on his profile and read it to her, letting her take a peek at the few photos he has. The same photos I've spent way too long staring at.

"Holy shit. Are those real?" She squints, leaning closer. "Because good lord. I swear I could wash my laundry on those bad boys. Specifically my panties."

"Ryan!"

"What? I'd wash yours too. How come there are no pictures of his face?"

I shrug. "I don't know. A lot of profiles are like that though."

"Doesn't that worry you?"

"Not really."

"Hockey Guy, huh?" she asks, still staring down at his abs. "But you hate sports. What's with you attracting dudes who like sports recently?"

"I know." I wrinkle my nose, setting my phone aside. "It's his one flaw. But we've clicked on other stuff, so I'm choosing to ignore that little passion of his."

"Does he play or just a fan?"

I snort. "Right, because a hockey player needs to get on some dating app to get a girl to date him."

"Hey, you never know. I saw a movie once where—"

"Ryan, we've talked about mixing up fairy tales and real life before."

She sticks her tongue out at my teasing. "Fine. Either way, I'm just glad you are *finally* going to go out with someone. It's been ages since you have."

"It hasn't been ages. Just…" I think back to the last time I did go on a date. *Oh crap.* "It's been like a year," I whisper.

She laughs. "Yeah, like I said, ages. You've been cooped up in your apartment being a badass girl boss and I think that's great, but you haven't been paying attention to your other needs." Her brows bounce up and down. "If you catch my drift."

"I take plenty care of myself, thank you very much."

"Sure, the vibe is great, but we both know the real thing is better."

"My vibrator always makes sure I come first."

She groans. "Ugh. That is the worst. They either rail into you like they're humping a couch or they can't find your clit. Um, sir, it is literally right there!"

"What? You mean it's not the fat roll on my thigh?"

"Does that feel good, baby?" she mocks in a deep voice. "I don't know, Brad. Does it feel good when I lick your belly button instead of your dick? Because that's about how far you are from my clit right now."

We fall into a fit of giggles, several people staring at us. I can't tell if it's our loud laughter or if it's Ryan they're all staring at, no doubt recognizing her from social media. That tends to happen often when we go out.

"We should date better men," Ryan says, composing herself. She tips her drink toward me. "Here's hoping your Hockey Guy takes care of all your needs."

"Ryan! I'm not going to sleep with him on the first date!"

"Hello, have you seen his abs? Maybe you need to look again." She reaches for my phone again and I snatch it away. "Boo!"

"You know what? Maybe *you* should find someone to date. You're clearly horny."

"I'm, uh, actually seeing Steven again tomorrow night at my showing," she says quietly. "You're still coming, right?"

Ugh. Steven.

He's a piece of work, and I don't understand what Ryan sees in him. He's an artsy type who is a little too heavy into the whole moody artist trope. To be frank, he's a dick, and Ryan deserves better.

"You know I'll be there. I can't wait to see Steven again." *And punch him right in the taint.*

Knowing my distaste for him, she laughs off my words, but I see the uncertainty in her own eyes.

"Anyway," she says, tossing her hair over her shoulder and resting her arms against the table. "I know how you can make it up to me."

"Make what up to you?"

"Not telling me about your *ab*solute"—she winks at her own joke—"hockey hottie."

"I told you, it was because—"

"You didn't want to jinx it, didn't know if it was going to be a thing...yeah, yeah." She waves off my excuses. "Just let me guilt-trip you, okay?"

"I don't think you're supposed to tell me you're guilt-tripping me."

"I got some tickets..."

"No!" I hold my hand up, shaking my head. "Nope. I know where this is going already."

"Come on, Harper, please!" She folds her hands together. "Please! You're my best friend in the whole wide world and I want to experience my first ever live hockey game with you."

"Where did you even get tickets to a hockey game? Are you even a hockey fan?"

"I like the butts."

Okay, that's fair.

"And remember those photographs I sold to that former pro-baseball player? I guess he's some sort of hotshot sports agent now and had some tickets to spare. I wasn't about to say no." She bats her lashes at me. "Please, Harper, please. It's this Friday and I really want to go."

"I hate sports. You know that."

"I do know that. But you know I hate when you hide things from me, and well"—she waves her hand across the table, sitting back in her chair with confidence— "look at us now."

Dammit.

"That's a low blow."

She lifts a shoulder. "Told you I'd guilt-trip you."

She did. She warned me.

"Fine," I say through gritted teeth. "Fine. But I plan to complain the entire time."

She grins triumphantly. "I would expect nothing less."

"Oh god."

A low moan escapes my lips, and I don't even care.

I pull my other shoe off and another moan slips free as I sink my toes into the soft rug, loving the feel under my aching feet. I'm not used to wearing real shoes for more than a quick errand, and I am definitely not used to wearing heels.

Ryan had a small showing at a gallery downtown, so I was peopling for the past four hours, which is way too long for me. I'm going to have to do the same thing tomorrow at the hockey game I'm being forced to attend.

I'm beat. And starving. The hors d'oeuvres they were serving were way too tiny.

I need food and a bed—in that order.

I make my way to my bedroom and don't feel an ounce of shame when I moan the moment my boobs fall out of my bra. I swap my jeans for pajama shorts and my silky blouse for an oversized shirt that has roughly twenty holes in it.

I'm scrubbing off the minimal amount of makeup I wore tonight when my phone buzzes against the counter.

I hurry to check it, hoping it's Wright and feeling like a fiend looking for my next thrill.

HockeyGuy69: Say I'm on the hunt for something tasty and need a pick-me-up in the morning. What's the best coffee shop in the city?

HorrorHarper: Mine.

．　．　．

HockeyGuy69: You own a coffee shop?

HorrorHarper: No. I make my own coffee.

HockeyGuy69: So let me get this straight—I ask for something tasty and you invite me over?

HockeyGuy69: Because if that's the case, the answer is yes.

I chuckle. Of course that's where he goes.

HorrorHarper: Slow your roll there, Mr. Romance.

HockeyGuy69: I'm sensing sarcasm regarding the name.

HorrorHarper: You've sensed right.

. . .

HorrorHarper: As for coffee, I have a whole coffee bar in my apartment and everything. Though Jennie's Java isn't too bad if you're in a pinch.

HockeyGuy69: A coffee bar? Like a booze bar but for coffee?

I head into my kitchen, snap a quick picture of my setup, and send it to him.

While I wait for his response, I rifle through my cabinets for food, but there's next to nothing in them and what I do have doesn't sound good at all.

I place an order for a sub from my favorite place just a few miles away, then grab a glass of wine and settle onto the couch while I wait.

HockeyGuy69: How Pinterest of you.

HorrorHarper: Don't poke fun. It's genius! I save SO much money doing it this way.

HockeyGuy69: I've always thought coffee was equivalent to sandwiches or salads—they always taste better when someone else makes them.

. . .

HorrorHarper: Sure. If you don't know what you're doing.

HockeyGuy69: I feel like you've just insulted my cooking abilities.

HorrorHarper: Sandwiches and salads don't count as cooking.

HockeyGuy69: That's fair. And to be honest, I don't really cook much anyway.

HorrorHarper: But you can cook, right? You just choose not to? Because a guy who can cook...wowza. *fans self*

HockeyGuy69: Cooking turns you on, huh?

HorrorHarper: Very much so.

. . .

HockeyGuy69: *signs up for cooking lessons*

HockeyGuy69: Honestly, though, sometimes my schedule doesn't afford me much time to mess around in the kitchen, so I often opt for takeout or prepared meals from the nutritionist.

HorrorHarper: Is "nutritionist" a code word for mom?

HockeyGuy69: I just spit out my beer and now all my buddies are looking at me weird.

HorrorHarper: You're out with friends right now?

HockeyGuy69: Unfortunately. I'd rather be at home, but I also kind of need to be here. It's a work thing.

HockeyGuy69: And no, I actually mean my nutritionist.

HorrorHarper: *whistles* Someone's fancy.

. . .

HockeyGuy69: Eh. Perks of the job.

HorrorHarper: I guess working in sports you would have access to things like that.

HorrorHarper: And no, that is not an invitation to start talking sports. I refuse to like them.

HockeyGuy69: We'll see about that.

HorrorHarper: Might as well quit while you're ahead. It's not going to happen.

HockeyGuy69: I can be very persuasive, you know.

HorrorHarper: Oh, I don't doubt that for a second.

HorrorHarper: Even though you don't show your face in your profile pictures, I'm willing to bet you have a stupid dimple in your stupid face and it gets you all the stupid things you want.

. . .

HockeyGuy69: Would you like some fries to go with that salt?

HorrorHarper: YES!

HorrorHarper: But only because I'm hungry and haven't had dinner yet.

HockeyGuy69: It's like 9 PM! That is way past nom-noms time.

HorrorHarper: Agreed. And if I don't get some nom-noms soon, I may rage.

HorrorHarper: I ordered some delivery.

HockeyGuy69: Please do not hurt the delivery person. I don't want to have to go to court and testify against you. I mean, like I said, I look really good in a suit, so I'd do it, but please don't make me.

. . .

HorrorHarper: You'd testify against me just to prove to everyone how good you look in a suit?

HockeyGuy69: 100%

Dots dance across the screen, then disappear.

It happens again.

Then again.

Hmm.

I set my phone aside, giving him time to figure out what he's clearly struggling to say. I give my attention to the TV I've had on for background noise.

I wish I could say that by the time the delivery person rings the bell and I buzz them up, pay, and then settle back down with my food, I've forgotten all about the dancing dots.

But I haven't.

Finally, when I'm halfway through my dinner, my phone buzzes again.

HockeyGuy69: I'm sorry I've been a little MIA lately.

HockeyGuy69: I don't want to give the lame excuse of work but…work. The hours kind of suck sometimes.

. . .

I trust his words, but something is telling me it's not the whole story.

I deserve the whole story.

HockeyGuy69: I'm sure you're asleep by now, but I just wanted you to know that.

HockeyGuy69: Good night, Harper.

I don't text him back.

CHAPTER 11

Turns out not thinking is really stupid.

Like monumentally dumb.

We have our first home game tonight and we're supposed to be preparing for it, but I can't focus.

All I can think about is how I'm going to explain to Harper who the hell I am.

On our date.

Date.

The one I asked her out on tomorrow night.

Stupid, stupid, stupid.

This app thing was supposed to help me find someone to *relax* with, not cause me more stress.

What the fuck have I gotten myself into?

"Pull your fucking head out of your ass, Wright!" Colter's voice cuts through my thoughts, and I glower over at the prick. "This season isn't all about you, Golden Boy."

Golden Boy? Not even close.

"Fuck off, Colter."

"*I* should fuck off?" He skates to a stop right in front of me, getting into my face. "How about *you* fuck off. You're the one dragging the team down."

"We've only lost one game."

Our first three games of the season have been away games, leaving us without the home-ice advantage, and the one game we lost went to overtime, so we still got a point. We're not exactly struggling out here.

"Yeah, no thanks to your shit playing."

I grit my teeth, trying not to let it show how much his words get to me.

That's the funny thing about hockey—your team can be winning game after game, but you can still be struggling. Dropped passes, shots missing the net by a mile, being outskated.

That's where I am right now. We're winning, but everyone else might as well be playing a different game than me. I'm screwing up basic things, and people are beginning to take notice. We can't keep this up all season, winning games by just a point, almost letting the other team score on simple mistakes.

I know it and everyone else knows it too. Playing like this isn't going to get me a contract extension, not by a long shot.

Colter inches closer, our noses nearly touching. "The only reason we won was because your ugly buddy Rhodes pulled your ass out of trouble. Scared Boston away with that ugly fucking scar of his."

"Fuck. Off." I growl again, my patience with the asshole wearing thin.

"Or what? Gonna have Rhodes come fight your battle for you again?" His lips pull into an ugly smile. "You don't have the fucking balls to hit me. You're weak, Wright. And if the captain wasn't so in love with you and didn't convince Coach you're worth the ice time, we both know I'd have your minutes in a heartbeat."

Ah. So that's what this is about.

He's jealous.

Which, given my piss-poor playing lately, is comical.

Rhodes skates closer in my periphery, and I shake my head at him, keeping him back.

This isn't his battle. It's mine.

I step toward my teammate. "Even at your absolute best, you couldn't handle the extra minutes."

And it's true. Colter is a selfish player, and that's what's holding him back. I might be shit right now, but he couldn't cut it. He'd be too busy trying to make fancy plays and costing us precious inches.

I might not be perfect out there, but I have years of experience and patience.

He shoves at me. "Fuck you, Wright."

I let him have that shove because I deserve it.

But he won't get another.

"You think you're untouchable, think your spot can't easily be filled. You're wrong."

Another shove, and I break.

The gloves come off, and I hear his nose crack under

my fist. He stumbles backward, then charges me again, getting my jaw good. The unique metallic flavor hits me all at once.

I run my tongue over my teeth and grin at him.

I like this.

Shit, maybe I even *needed* this.

Colter goes for another blow and misses. He pulls at my sweater, trying to yank it over my head, but I'm bigger than him and easily wrench myself away, landing another hit to his jaw.

Around and around we go. Back and forth, swinging in circles now, matching each other blow for blow.

Nobody around us moves until we hit the ice, then suddenly they're all pulling at us.

Rhodes grabs under my arms, hauling me up and off Colter, who scrambles to get out of Miller's grasp to reach for me again.

"Enough!" Lowell yells, a hand on each of our chests, shoving us away from one another. "Fucking enough. Cool off."

Miller tries to drag Colter away, and he shoves at him —which pisses me off all over again—then skates toward the dressing room.

We all hear the doors slam as he makes his way down the tunnel.

Lowell looks over at me. "You good?" I nod. "Good. Don't pull that shit again." When he's skating past me, he mutters, "Been wanting to do that since day one."

The laugh that's on my lips is cut short when I catch Coach's eye from across the ice.

He's not happy.

Not fucking happy at all.

Awesome.

Colter doesn't come back—which doesn't matter to me—and the rest of the morning is uneventful.

We're in the dressing room when Rhodes flops down onto the bench next to me.

"All right. Spill it."

"What are you talking about?"

He presses a hard finger into the pinched skin between my eyebrows. "I'm talking about that shit. I'm supposed to be the broody one."

I smack his hand away. "Piss off."

"Not until you tell me what's going on."

"It's nothing."

He's quiet for a moment, and I think he's going to let it go.

But he's Rhodes, so of course he's not.

Instead, he leans down, tipping his head toward mine, and speaks low. "We have a game tonight, you know. So you better start talking before your head is so far up your own ass that we lose and your contract with the Comets turns to ashes right in front of you."

Shit.

He's right, and I hate that he's right.

I gnash my teeth, trying to rein in my frustration.

"Fine."

I tell him about Harper. How we met…then met again. How I left out some minor details like the fact that I play professional hockey. How I haven't told her that HockeyGuy69 is also the guy she played an awful game of nighttime "I spy" with.

When I'm finished, he just stares at me, mouth slackened, eyes wide.

"Are you…are you like extra dumb or something? Concussed?" He places his hand against my forehead. "Are you sick?"

I swat him away again. "I'm fine."

"If you're pulling shit like this, clearly you're not. What the hell, man? Why?"

"I don't know. I just…*fuck*!" I run a hand through my sweaty hair. "She's not into sports and doesn't have a clue who I am. Doesn't care at all." I shrug. "It's nice to not worry about all that for a change."

Rhodes shakes his head. "I hate how that actually makes sense to me."

"See? I'm not completely nuts."

"No. You are. What the hell were you going to tell her when you met her, huh? Just hoped she'd laugh it off and you two would bone and that'd be it?"

I clench my fists at the thought of that being it.

"I was hoping she'd understand, yes."

"You know the likelihood of that is almost nonexistent, right? Are you really sure this is what you want to do? It's not too late to back out. You haven't gone on the date yet."

"I'm not going to ghost her like some asshole."

"You have no problem lying to her like one."

Another squeeze of my fists.

"Face it—you're fucked."

"You think I don't know that?" I huff out a derisive laugh. "If this was supposed to be some pep talk, you suck."

"Yeah, well, I didn't think you'd tell me this shit. I just figured it was Colter being a cock again or that look Coach gave you after the fight." He crosses his arms over his chest, leaning back against his cubby. "Damn, dude. No wonder you're playing like shit, missing easy passes and not having your head in the game. You're all messed up from this."

We sit in silence for a few minutes, a few straggling teammates shuffling about.

I don't know why I asked Harper out, like shit isn't complicated enough already.

Okay, that's a lie.

I know exactly why I did it—I like her. Probably a lot more than I'm allowing myself to admit.

But I could have found a better way for her to find out it's me. I could have just been honest from the beginning too, but it's too late for that.

Now I have to figure out how the hell I'm going to fix it all.

If this were any other chick, some random hookup, it wouldn't be a big deal because it wouldn't mean anything.

But Harper…she means something.

"You know you have to tell her before your date, right?"

"I know."

"She's gonna flip."

"I know."

"You're an idiot."

"I know."

"I—"

"You're not helping," I cut him off, glaring. "I'll tell her, okay? I'll fucking tell her."

"When?"

It's a simple word, but the meaning behind it is anything but.

What he really means is *before tonight*.

He wants me at the game with a clear conscience.

I *need* to be at the game with a clear conscience.

"I'll tell her," I promise quietly.

"Good."

There's nothing like playing in front of a home crowd. There's a buzz in your veins and in the air.

Tonight, mine is buzzing for a different reason.

I head for the dressing room, trying to block everything out.

Several heads swivel my way, probably because of my busted lip and the bruise on my jaw after the fight with Colter this morning.

I keep my head down as I change out of my suit into some shorts and a t-shirt, then pop my earbuds in and settle onto the couch we have in the lounge. I pull my phone from my pocket and turn on a random '90s playlist to try to relax.

My eyes drift toward the BeeMine app.

I tried several times to message Harper earlier, but everything I typed out sounded horrible.

There is no doubt she's going to be pissed. She may never forgive me or talk to me again.

And I'd deserve that one hundred percent.

But Rhodes was right. I need to tell her.

If I don't, it's all I'm going to be thinking about tonight, and I can*not* be thinking about that tonight.

If that fight with Colter this morning taught me anything, it's that I can't keep screwing up.

I want to be better than that. Better than *him*.

I click on the app and pull up my messages with Harper.

HockeyGuy69: There's something I need to tell you.

. . .

HockeyGuy69: It's probably going to piss you off, but I have to clear the air.

HockeyGuy69: I'm Collin.

HockeyGuy69: Collin Wright. And I play for the NHL.

CHAPTER 12

HockeyGuy69: There's something I need to tell you.

A pit forms in my stomach as I read his words.

We didn't talk last night and I've tried hard all day to not think much about it, but I won't lie—it's been eating at me.

Ever since he asked me out, something has seemed…off.

I don't know if it's nerves or if he's actually just busy with work, but it's off nonetheless.

Another message comes through.

HockeyGuy69: It's probably going to piss you off, but I have to clear the air.

Oh crap, here it comes.

"Nope!" Ryan steals my phone away just as it vibrates again. She slips it into the abyss known as her purse as we make our way down the arena stairs to our seats. "That's mine for the night. No more pining over Hockey Hottie. Tonight is girls' night."

I should protest. Should tell her that's a stupid rule.

But I can't bring myself to say it because I'm not so sure I want to hear what he has to say.

Does he want to bail on the date? Has he been catfishing me all along? I mean, he's seemed too good to be true from day one, so I wouldn't be entirely surprised.

"Here we are," Ryan says, scooting down the aisle. She claps her hands, bouncing up and down with excitement. "Holy shit. These seats are amazing!"

I want to point out that since she's never been to a hockey game before, she doesn't know if these seats actually are good.

But considering we're just three rows back from the glass, I'd say her assumption is correct.

Ryan forced us to arrive nearly an hour before puck drop. She claimed she wanted to make sure we got to our seats okay, but I know she just didn't want to miss warmups.

She also promised snacks if I agreed to it.

"So when do we get to the good part?"

"Well, apparently they do warmups and then there's a bit of a break and—" She pauses, then snorts out a laugh when she catches my bored expression. "Oh. You meant food."

"You promised popcorn. Nachos too."

"And alcohol."

"All the alcohol."

She chuckles. "All right. I'll be right back. But no nachos until later."

"Because that's the only way you're going to get me to stay the entire game?"

A grin. "You know me so well."

She takes off for the food, leaving me sitting there with nothing to do since my phone is in her purse.

Spectators begin to file in around me. A woman sits a few seats down, and I can hear her on the phone talking about something to do with goats. There's nobody in the two rows in front of us yet.

I still can't believe we're sitting this close to the ice. I once went to a football game with my dad and we were so far from the field you could barely make out the players. Here…it's going to be like I can reach out and touch them.

And it's chilly too.

I pull my cardigan closed a little more, shivering a bit at the nip in the air.

"First time?" the woman asks, drawing my attention.

"How'd you know?"

She nods toward where I have my arms crossed over me. "I was the same way my first game. But you get used to it."

"I really didn't think I'd be this chilly, but I should have known. I'm a wimp when it comes to the cold."

She laughs. "Me too. It'll warm up once more bodies get in here, but not enough to take your cardi off."

A shadow falls over her and a beer appears in front of her face. She grins at the tall guy with ink-black hair and black-framed glasses who takes the seat next to her. He's wearing a shirt that says "G.O.A.T. Dad" with a picture of him and several tiny goats. I'm not usually into the whole nerd-vibe thing he has going, but this guy is...wow.

She takes the drink from his outstretched hand, then tips the cup my way. "Plus, the alcohol helps. I'm Delia, by the way." She gestures toward the guy beside her. "This is my husband, Zach. Please ignore his embarrassing shirt. He wouldn't take it off."

He leans around her and sends me a grin. "She's always trying to get me naked."

She swats at him. "Zachary!"

I laugh. "I'm Harper. It's nice to meet you both."

"Are you here for the Comets or the Caps? I assume Comets since you're in season ticket seats."

"Uh, Comets. I'm just here for the snacks mostly."

They laugh like I'm joking.

I'm not.

"Oh my gosh," Ryan says, dropping back down into the seat next to me. "You should have seen the lines out there. It was like all of a sudden people came from nowhere. I'm so glad we got here when we did. I heard someone in line say that warmups start—"

The players come barreling onto the ice.

"Well, right now, I guess."

She does another little clap, watching as they move across the rink.

They look…kind of beautiful if I'm being honest.

The way they move is breathtaking. It's smooth, like they're gliding on air.

She hands me a few napkins. "Here. For your drool. And the popcorn."

I scowl at her. "I'm not drooling."

"Sure you're not." She winks, then hands me a beer. "These were free, by the way."

"Ryan, did you flirt your way into getting free drinks?"

"Of course I did. Have you seen the prices here?" She shrugs, turns around, and waves at a guy sitting a few rows up. "Plus he was cute," she says, turning back my way with a flirty grin.

I shake my head at her, then return my gaze to the ice.

A few Comets players are skating around in circles on one half. A few are doing some sort of stretch that makes them look like they're humping the ground, and a few…

A body slams into the glass, causing me to jump, spilling beer down my secondhand Aerosmith t-shirt and the cardigan I'm wearing.

"Son of a…" I shoot up from my seat, cold, sticky liquid clinging to me.

"Oh, crap!" Ryan grabs a handful of napkins and

starts patting at my shirt. "Dammit. I love this shirt too. I—"

There's a tap on the glass that pulls our attention.

One of the players—who has a mean, jagged scar across his face—mouths *Sorry* to us. He taps his buddy on the shoulder, pulling his attention our way.

The moment our eyes collide, I freeze.

He gapes at me, his eyes—which I can now see are a clear green—wide with shock.

"Collin?"

"Wait, like Hot Hitchhiker Collin?" Ryan asks.

I don't answer her. I'm too busy staring at the guy I never thought I'd see again.

His friend says something quietly to him, and Collin nods without looking over. He can't seem to take his eyes off me either.

We're locked in a trance, unable to move.

Then someone calls his name from across the ice, and just like that, it's broken.

He turns and I gasp.

Wright.

It's there, stitched clear as day on the back of his jersey, along with the number 96.

I actually meant to type in 96, but I guess we'll call it a happy accident.

He nods at whoever spoke to him, then turns back to me. He takes a step closer and his teammate pulls at his arm, trying to drag him away.

Even from here, I can see that his eyes are full of so many emotions—shock, worry, regret.

Another tug from his teammate, and this time Collin allows himself to be pulled away.

He looks back at me three times on his way to the other side of the ice, and each time it feels like a punch to the stomach.

Then he disappears down a tunnel and I'm left standing here feeling like a complete fool.

"Give me my phone," I say to Ryan, finding my voice once he's gone.

She reaches into her purse without question and hands it over.

I hold my breath as I click on the notification from the BeeMine app, hoping this is all some sort of sick coincidence.

It's not.

It's right there, his confession.

This is what he wanted to talk about.

HockeyGuy69: I'm Collin.

HockeyGuy69: Collin Wright. And I play for the NHL.

"Holy shit." I exhale heavily.

"What? Is that really Hot Hitchhiker?"

"Ryan…" I shove the phone in her face. "It's Hot Hockey Guy too."

"What? No it's not." She grabs the phone from my hands as I drop back down into my seat. Her jaw drops when she reads his text. "Oh my god. It's…"

"Yeah."

"Holy shit."

"Yeah."

"This is…*wow*."

She sits beside me, scrolling through our messages. I don't even care enough at this point to stop her. It doesn't matter anymore. Our whole relationship is a lie anyway.

"I can't believe this. You had no idea?"

"No! I don't sport. I couldn't tell you the first thing about hockey. I thought the puck was made of plastic."

"It's rubber," Ryan corrects. "Everyone knows that."

"I didn't! That's how much I don't sport!"

She tucks her lips together, trying not to laugh.

But it doesn't work. She bursts into a fit of giggles, and before I know it, I'm joining her.

I'm almost certain people are staring at us, but I don't care.

It feels good to laugh, and if I don't laugh, I might cry.

My hitchhiker is my hockey guy.

His name is Collin Wright, and he plays for the NHL.

What hell am I supposed to do with that?

"Do you want to go?" Ryan asks during the break between the first and second period.

Part of me wanted to leave the moment I saw Collin on the ice.

But there's another part of me that can't seem to walk away now.

He was right—seeing the game live is so much better than seeing it on TV.

There's something exhilarating about hearing the bodies crash against the boards. Something so thrilling about hearing the puck ping off the crossbar. And watching the players glide down the ice effortlessly like they aren't playing a high-speed game on frozen water with knives attached to their feet? It's intoxicating.

Too bad it's all being overshadowed by the fact that Collin lied to me.

Twice.

Sports industry.

That's what he told me, and he said it twice.

Really, I should have realized it then.

But if not then, I should have seen the other hints too. I spent the time before puck drop scrolling back through all our messages, picking them apart.

Wright lobbied for Freddy Krueger, just like Collin did.

He's twenty-seven, just like Collin.

Hell, he even tried to convince me to like sports, just like Collin.

And even though he admitted he was a hockey fan, he skirted around the topic often enough that I should have picked up on him trying to hide something.

I'm so embarrassed.

He must have thought it was hilarious, pretending to be a different person. Pretending we didn't meet before. Pretending I didn't hold his fucking sauce as he dunked his chicken nuggets.

That's the part that hurts the most I think. He knew it was me. It's not like I hid my name or my identity behind faceless photos. I was upfront from the beginning. He never was.

And yeah, okay…I understand it to an extent. He's a professional athlete who is likely making millions of dollars a year. He's going to want to be a bit private.

But it's me.

I don't care about his status. I just like him.

Liked, I remind myself.

Past tense.

"No," I tell Ryan. "We can stay."

"Are you sure?" She's trapped her lip between her teeth, her brows drawn tightly together as she studies me closely.

"I'm sure. But I could definitely use more alcohol."

"Want me to go?"

I shake my head. "No, I got it. I could use the fresh air."

She nods and lets me out of the aisle.

I squeeze past several fans, taking note of the number of people wearing WRIGHT on their backs. A few of them look at me and I swear I feel their judgment, like they know and agree with how dumb I am for not putting two and two together before.

The line for booze is long, and I don't make it back until right before the start of the second period.

"You totally missed the little kiddos sliding around on the ice," Ryan says as I hand her one of the three beers I got. "I guess they're called Mites or something. Anyway, they were so adorable."

She doesn't comment on the extra beer like the good friend she is.

What she does say is "I'm sorry."

"For what?"

"For pushing you to get on that app. If you hadn't, maybe you wouldn't be feeling like you are now."

Leave it to Ryan to not miss a thing.

"I feel like a fool," I say quietly.

"I know. But you're not the fool—he is. He's the one who tricked you."

"Yeah, but if I had just paid a bit more attention, maybe I could have connected the dots."

"Like you said, you don't sport." She grins at the words. "How are you supposed to know anything about something you don't follow? That would be like me trying to piece together anything about horror movies. Not my pig, not my farm, you know."

171

I suppose she's right.

The announcer says something over the intercom and the crowd goes wild, cheering loudly as the players make their way onto the ice.

The game starts again, twenty minutes on the clock.

Collin's out there, staying back by the blue line that's not too far from where we're seated.

The way he moves…it's incredible. I have no idea how I missed him being an athlete before. There's such focus and precision in every move he makes.

His brows are drawn together in concentration as he watches the puck move from stick to stick, his mouth pulled into a thin line. He's completely focused on the game, and it's riveting to watch. I have no idea how he's drowning out the noise of the crowd, but it's like we're not even here.

He gets the puck, then sends it sailing over to the other side of the ice, to the guy with the scar on his lip.

Rhodes, his jersey reads, with a big number 6 right below it.

His partner sends the puck right back, and Collin shoots.

The crowd erupts around us as the red light ignites.

He scored!

Everyone is jumping up and down, the sound deafening. We get on our feet too, pumping our fists in the air.

Collin's back hits the glass as his teammates crowd around him, patting his back, bumping his fists.

They're right by us, several people beating on the glass with zeal.

It's all so…electrifying.

Just as Collin's about to skate away, he turns…and looks directly at me.

Then winks.

I swear I melt into my seat.

The Comets win 4-2, and though Collin doesn't score again, he earns what I learn is called an assist.

The arena is buzzing with excitement, and fans are thrilled to have seen Collin score. I heard a few people talking about how the team lost the Stanley Cup last year and saying it was Collin's fault, so they're glad to see him making a comeback.

I also thought I heard the word *arrest* mentioned, but I'm sure I'm mistaken about that.

"Okay, it's official: I'm a hockey fan," Ryan says, staring out at the ice longingly as the players leave it.

"Are you a hockey fan, or do you just like looking at the hockey players?"

"Yes." She sighs dreamily. "Like, I'm not going to lie, I am totally horny right now."

I wouldn't admit it, but same.

And it's not even about the players.

It's *everything* about the game. The speed, the buzz, the power they exude. It's all just so…*hot*.

"Come on, let's go stand up next to the glass."

She grabs my hand, dragging me down the few rows before I can protest. A couple of other people are down there too, clapping and cheering still, and she wedges us in between them so we can see.

"Ladies and gentlemen, your three stars of the game!" the announcer calls in that exaggerated voice all announcers have. "For our third star, with the first goal of the game, we have number 13, Grady Miller!"

There are whistles and shouts of joy as the player takes the ice, makes a circle, and then disappears again, but not before handing his stick off to a kid hanging over the railings.

"For our second star of the night, with the game-winning goal, we have number 6, Adrian Rhodes!"

The crowd cheers as Collin's partner skates back out onto the ice, lifting his stick and making a short circle before heading back off. He also gives his stick to a young fan.

"And our first star of the game, coming off a tough season last year but more than making up for it with a goal *and* an assist, we have number 96, Collin Wright!"

Everyone is on their feet as Collin skates back out. He does a few quick circles, then hands his stick to someone standing over by the tunnel. He leans in to talk to the person, pointing in the direction where we're standing.

Alarm bells begin to sound in my head and I pull at Ryan, trying to get her to leave with me.

"No," she says, dragging me back down. "Definite

no."

"Ryan, come on."

"Shh! He's gonna talk."

She points up at the jumbotron. The camera is focused on Collin as he slides onto a bench, sitting beside some guy with a microphone. He's breathing hard, his helmet off, hair sticking up everywhere.

And still, somehow, he looks amazing.

Maybe even better than before.

There's a sheen of sweat covering his face and his cheeks are red from exertion, but damn does he still look lickable.

Ryan snorts from beside me. "You got that right."

Oh crap. I must have said that out loud.

"Collin, wow," the interviewer says. "What a night for you, huh?"

"I just got out there and played hockey, you know," Collin answers.

"Oh my god. You never told me his voice was that deep."

Ryan's practically drooling, and I can't blame her one bit.

"I bet it had to feel good putting up a goal and an assist after the Game Six loss last season and the off-season drama that happened afterward."

Collin chuckles, a grin that might look playful to others pulling at his lips. That's not his real smile though. I know that for a fact.

"That's one word for it," he says.

"Now, Collin, it's no secret that you've been struggling a bit this season so far. We know it's still early on, but preseason was a bit of a mess. What changed for you tonight?"

Collin's eyes flit across the ice.

I peel my eyes off the screen, and for the third time tonight, our gazes collide.

"Just had better focus. Something to prove, you know."

"And prove it you did." The interviewer laughs like he just made the funniest joke in the world. "All right, Collin, we'll let you get back to your teammates. Thanks for talking with us for a moment, and congrats again on the win tonight."

"Thanks, J.P."

Collin shakes the guy's hand, then heads off the bench and down the tunnel.

The interviewer continues to talk, but I tune him out.

Ryan squeals next to me. "Holy crap, Harper. He is…" She fans herself. "Hot. So fucking hot."

"Too bad he's a liar."

"Crap." A frown pulls at her lips. "I forgot about that part. Ready to get out of here?"

"Please."

"Drinks?"

"God yes."

She laughs, linking her arm with mine, dragging me up the steps.

"Miss Harper?" someone calls out.

I spin back around to find a man standing there, holding a stick.

"Um…yes?"

"This is from Mr. Wright. He specifically asked that it be delivered to you."

"To…me?"

"Yes, ma'am."

I'm acutely aware people are staring at us right now. This man with that hockey stick, trying to hand it off to me. Me just standing there with a dropped jaw, trying to wrap my head around it.

"Harper," Ryan says quietly. "Just take it. People are staring."

"He insisted, ma'am," the guy says, shaking the stick.

"I…okay," I say quietly, curling my fingers around it. "Thank you."

"Have a good evening, ma'am."

The guy scurries away, leaving me standing there with a long, heavy piece of equipment in my hand.

"Did…that just happen?" Ryan asks.

"I think so." I grasp it warily. I've never held a hockey stick before. "It's much bigger than I anticipated."

"And I sincerely hope that's what you're saying when you get him into bed."

"Ryan!"

"What?" She shrugs. "It's the romantic in me." She tugs at me. "Now come on. There's a bar around the corner. Let's drink and figure out how we're going to handle this."

CHAPTER 13

COLLIN

"Dude! Yes!" Rhodes says as I enter the dressing room after all the press meetings. He pats me hard on the back, and I cough up the water I was chugging. "Fucking yes! That's the shit we need out there all season, man."

He's ecstatic, grinning as much as Rhodes grins.

"Yeah, yeah. You scored too," I remind him.

"Yeah, but you needed it more than I did."

I did need it. So fucking badly.

I'm hyped I scored.

To have Coach look at me with pride instead of worry, to have my teammates who have been on the fence about me looking at me like I'm not a complete failure…it feels so damn good.

But I can't get that look on Harper's face out of my head.

"What's wrong? Your face just totally dropped. You— oh. Shit. The girl."

"Harper."

"Who's Harper? And more importantly, does she

have anything to do with your game tonight?" Lowell asks, flopping down beside me. "Because if so, keep her ass around."

"She's…"

Well, fuck. Is she the girl who nearly ran me over? The girl I've been messaging? The girl I'm supposed to be going on a date with tomorrow? Or is she just someone I barely knew?

I settle on "It's complicated."

"Yeah, well, *un*complicate it. We need your head in the game like it was tonight. Need that magic. And if she's it, fix it."

Fucking hockey players and their superstitions.

Some of us tape our own stick before each game. Some want to be the last off of the ice. Some have special routines they need to follow.

We all have something.

Truthfully, it crossed my mind for a millisecond that I scored because of Harper.

She's the only difference I've made.

Maybe…maybe she is my good luck charm.

Rhodes clears his throat, and I glance up at him.

"Fix it for the reasons not running around in your head right now."

I sigh. He's right…again.

Asshole.

"I hear you," I tell him.

Lowell's gaze bounces between the two of us, trying to figure out what's going on.

"Slapshots tonight, boys," Miller says, coming over to join us. He claps his hands together, probably still buzzing from the game. "Gotta celebrate those two points for our favorite geezer."

Lowell sends him a murderous glare. "I'm older than him and take great offense to that, so I will end you."

"I'm shaking." Miller rolls his eyes, completely unfazed by the captain's threat.

"Need I remind you, I'm older than all of you by a long shot," Smith, one of our centers, says from down the bench.

He's one of those dudes who has been in the NHL for years and a guy you want on your team. He doesn't make fancy plays and gets the job done, a background player you never hear much about but who holds a team together a lot more than most realize.

Miller's eyes are wide as he stares up at the six-foot-six giant. "Crap. Now I really am shaking."

We all laugh at the rookie.

"I'm down for Slapshots," Lowell says. "I can never sleep after a win anyway."

"Rhodes, you in?"

He looks over at me before he commits, and I shrug. "Why not?"

"Fuck it," Rhodes says. "I'm in too. But Lowell is buying us all beers."

"I am?"

"Yep." Rhodes slaps him on the back. "Don't worry, I've seen your AAV—you can afford it."

The moment we walked into Slapshots, we were bombarded with fans who were hungry for our attention. We gave our best press smiles and made our way through the crowd to find a quiet table in the back.

Rod drops off our usual drinks, sending a clear *Leave them be* message to the crowd with a deadly look, and save for a few of the drunker fans stumbling over now and again, it works.

We've only been here for twenty minutes, and I think I check my phone at least twice a minute.

Did Harper not see my number scrawled across the stick?

Did she see it and just not care?

I hold my breath as I click on the BeeMine app, expecting to find that we've been unmatched.

We haven't.

All of our messages are right there.

I type out a few different things.

I fucked up.

Delete.

I'm an idiot.

Delete.

I'm sorry.

Send.

. . .

"All right, man, what's with the obsessive phone checking? Oh, crap—what dumbass thing did you say during press this time?"

I flip Lowell off and he laughs.

I might have a bit of a reputation for accidentally cursing during the live press meetings or saying something I shouldn't. I keep telling Coach to keep me away from the camera, but he never listens.

"It's a girl," Miller says, peeking over my shoulder to see what I'm looking at. "It's gotta be. I see that BeeMine app on his phone. I don't get it. You're a hotshot hockey player—you can get laid any time you want."

I catch Lowell's eyes from across the table. He doesn't ask why I'm on the app, probably because he understands it without me saying anything.

We all used to be like Miller once: young, dumb, excited about women throwing themselves at us. Then we got older and jaded and more cautious. Given how the last relationship Lowell was in went, I know he understands.

"It's nothing," I mutter.

"Yeah, definitely a girl. I bet—"

My phone buzzes and I check it faster than a middle schooler waiting to hear from their crush.

Shep Clark: Fucking nice job tonight. Good to have you back.

. . .

I shoot him back a quick text, then lay my phone down with a sigh.

When I glance back up, all the guys are staring at me.

"What?" I bark.

Lowell laughs, Miller doesn't say shit, and Rhodes just shakes his head.

"It's not a chick. It's—Harper?"

She's sitting across the bar, her head bent low, giggling at something her friend—the same girl from her profile pictures—says.

I can't believe it's her.

I can't believe she was at my game tonight.

I can't believe she's here. Right here. In this bar.

A body steps in front of her table, blocking her from my view.

The dude steps in way too close, resting his elbows on the table, ignoring all her cues as she shrinks away from him.

He turns, and I swear I see red.

I'd know that ugly fucker anywhere.

It's Colter.

I'm out of my seat and crossing the bar before I know what I'm doing, the guys yelling at my back. I ignore them because there is no fucking way I am leaving her alone with him.

He's a slimy shit and I don't trust him.

Harper catches my eye as I approach, and I can already see the relief flashing in her gaze.

I don't bother sparing Colter a glance as I wrap my arm around her and say, "There you are."

She sinks into me, and I don't know if it's for show or if it's her body acting on its own; either way, I like it entirely too much.

"I tried texting you." I lift my brows as if to say *Just go with it.* "We're back in the corner." I flick my eyes to my teammate. "Oh, hey, Colter. Didn't see you there."

His eyes bounce between me and Harper. "Uh, you two know each other?"

"Yep." I pull her in closer, planting a kiss on her temple. "Thanks for checking in with her, but I got it from here." I look down at Harper. "Come on, ladies. Don't want the douchebags bothering you for too long."

Harper rolls her lips together, trying not to laugh, and her friend grabs her drink, looking more than happy to leave Colter behind too.

I pull Harper behind me toward the back of the bar, trying not to think too much about how good her hand feels in mine.

She tugs on it, stopping me when we're nearly there.

"We're in the clear." She slips her hand away, and I instantly miss the warmth. We nearly collide when I turn to face her and she startles, glaring up at me. "Thanks for the rescue."

"That guy had total slimeball vibes," her friend says. She juts out a hand between us. "Hi, I'm Ryan."

I clasp her hand in mine. "Nice to meet you, Ryan. I'm—"

"Oh," she interrupts, squeezing my hand tighter. "I know who you are. You're an ass."

I look to Harper for help, but she just lifts her brows as if to say *Yeah, what she said.*

"I don't disagree," I tell Ryan, pulling my hand back. I want to shake it out because damn did she have a strong grip, but I don't want to give her the satisfaction. I turn to Harper. "Can we talk?"

"I—"

"Yes," Ryan answers for her. She points at the table with Lowell, Miller, and Rhodes. "I'm going to find my future husband. You two go talk."

She gives Harper a look that I have no idea how to interpret and sashays toward the table.

"Evening, boys," I hear her say, sliding into the chair I abandoned.

They all perk up at her presence, ready to salivate over her.

Not that I blame them. Ryan is gorgeous.

But she's not Harper.

I turn back to find her peering up at me with wary eyes.

I dip my head toward the bar. "Want to sit?"

She doesn't answer, just gives me a curt nod and leads the way.

We settle in on two stools, and I signal for Rod. I don't normally have more than one or two drinks when we go out during the season, but tonight I can tell I'm going to need several.

He brings me over a beer and drops off another of whatever Harper's having.

I tip my drink back and take a long pull, letting the alcohol do its thing. I wipe my mouth on the back of my hand and peek over at Harper. Her fingers are wrapped around her straw and she's stirring her drink, staring down at it like it contains all the answers to life's questions.

I run a hand through my hair and spin toward her. "Look, Harper, I—"

"Hey, man! Sweet fucking goal tonight," a guy says, stumbling way too far into my space.

"Thanks," I reply curtly, inching away. I give my attention to Harper. "I—"

"Oh, man. Who do we have here?" the guy interrupts, leaning into Harper's face this time. "Damn, you're hot."

He reaches out like he's going to touch her, and I snap.

I shoot to my feet and grab the guy by the collar, tugging him up to his tiptoes.

I faintly hear the scraping of chairs over the floor and I have no doubt it's the guys, ready to back me up if needed.

There are several people around us, staring in surprise, waiting to see what happens.

I yank the drunken idiot closer. "Don't even think about putting your hands on her, or anyone else for that matter."

He lifts his hands in the air, eyes wide with shock. "I-I-I—"

"Fucking got it?" I growl.

The guy bobs his head up and down several times, swallowing thickly. "Y-Yeah, man. S-Sorry."

"Apologize to her, not me."

He looks over at Harper, fear in his eyes. "S-Sorry, miss. Had a few too m-many."

"Not a fucking excuse." I drop him back to his feet and he stumbles a bit. "Now go. Sober the fuck up."

"Shit, man," he murmurs as he scurries to leave. "Think I already have."

I stare him down until he disappears into the crowd.

"Good?" Rhodes calls out.

"Swear I am so wet right now," I hear Ryan say.

I drop back onto the stool, ignoring them all.

"Are you okay?" I ask Harper.

"That's twice."

"Huh?"

"That you've rescued me tonight. That's twice."

"Oh." I shrug. "It's not a big deal."

She just nods, then takes a sip of her drink.

An uncomfortable silence falls between us, and I hate it. I miss that level of comfort we had in the car together. That easy conversation we had when we were messaging.

I don't like whatever this is, and I know it's all my fault.

"I'm sorry," I finally say, breaking the tension.

She whips her head toward me, a deep crease between her brows. "You're sorry?"

"Yes."

"For what part?" She waves her hands, giving me the floor. "Go on. Elaborate for me. Tell me what you're sorry for exactly."

I open my mouth to explain things, but nothing comes out, the words frozen on my tongue.

She scoffs. "Of course. You're sorry but you can't admit what you did wrong." She shakes her head. "Let's try: Harper, I'm sorry I didn't tell you who I am that night in the car. Sure, we had over four hours together and I could have mentioned it at any point, but instead, I chose to lie about it. Or: I'm sorry that when I found your profile on a dating app, instead of just messaging you and saying who I am like a normal person, I lied and led you on for weeks. Or maybe even: I'm sorry I let you believe I was a good guy. By the way, I have two arrests for assault. Try any of those, *Collin*."

She spits my name out like it's the most disgusting thing she's ever heard.

And honestly, she has every right to feel that way.

I deserve it.

Everything she said is true, and her ire is warranted.

That doesn't make it sting any less.

"I'm sorry I didn't tell you who I was at first. It's… Well, I've had people take advantage of me before because of who I am, and I didn't know if I could trust you. And yeah, I should have told you who I was when I found you on BeeMine. But the lie by *omission*," I say pointedly because it wasn't an outright lie, causing her to roll her eyes, "was already set in stone at that point."

She opens her mouth to say something, but I cut her off.

"And, I just want to point out, I was arrested for assault twice but was only found guilty once."

"Is that supposed to make it okay?"

"Well, no. But it's not like I just jumped someone for shits and giggles. I had my reasons."

She waits for me to explain my side of things.

I don't talk about it a lot, mostly because I've never had to with it being expunged. Now that it's out there, I've still stayed tightlipped because at the end of the day, it won't matter why I did it. They're going to believe whatever they want anyway.

But with Harper...I want to set the record straight with her.

I lean in close, and unlike with the other two men to get in her space tonight, she doesn't shy away. She leans closer, too.

She smells like fresh, crisp apples, and I just happen to love apples.

"Remember my brother I told you about?"

"You mean the brother *Wright* told me about?"

I grind my teeth together, irritated with myself.

"Yeah." I clear my throat. "Anyway, the shit when I was younger was about him. Some people in small-town Kansas didn't take too well to the fact that he's gay. After some kids assaulted him and the school board turned a blind eye to it, I took matters into my own hands. Nobody wanted to believe or cared about what happened to the queer kid, so it was me who got in trouble. I was sixteen. I got adjudicated for assault, got one year of probation, had to pay restitution, got a hug from my brother and a cake from my parents. The other kids? They didn't get shit for what they did." I shake my head, disgusted by the treatment they received, like they were fucking untouchable. "As soon as I could, I had it expunged from my record, but once the media got hold of it…" I lift a shoulder. "It didn't matter anymore."

She regards me for a moment, eyes flitting across my face, over the cut on my lip from my scuffle with Colter this morning.

I'm sure to her I look like nothing but a hothead.

But I refuse to apologize for sticking up for my brother. I'd do it all over again in a heartbeat. Just like I'd punch out that guy who was touching that woman without her permission.

"Thank you for telling me that," she says quietly. "Your brother is lucky to have you."

Her words surprise me and a knot forms in my throat, though I'm not sure why. I swallow them down with a nod.

"How'd you hear about the arrests anyway?"

"Some people were making comments at the game and…"

"You ran to Google?"

"Ryan did."

I like that she has someone looking out for her. That's good.

"Ryan seems...fun."

For the first time since our night in the car, Harper gives me a genuine smile.

I didn't realize how badly I needed it either.

"She's the best. Truly. Forces me out of my shell, maybe a little too much sometimes."

She looks away, her attention back on her drink as she twists her straw between her fingers, that silence I'm really beginning to hate falling over us once more.

It lasts and lasts...and lasts some more.

Unable to take it any longer, I open my mouth to speak, but she beats me to it.

I look over to find her staring up at me with an intense gaze. "I'm really mad at you, Collin."

I expel a heavy breath and mirror her pose. "I know you are."

"I hate being lied to. It's kind of a deal-breaker for me."

"Kind of?" She nods. "Well, good."

Her brows knit together and she tips her head to the side. "It's a good thing it's a deal-breaker?"

"It's a good thing it's *kind of* a deal-breaker. That means there's room for me to convince you otherwise."

There's a hint of a smile at the corner of her mouth, but it's gone as fast as it appeared. She traps her bottom lip between her teeth, like she's trying to fight the grin that wants to break free. Like she's trying to tamp down what she's feeling.

Before I realize what I'm doing, I reach over and pluck it free, running the pad of my thumb over the indention her teeth have left.

Her breath is warm against my skin, her blue eyes wide with surprise.

I trace her soft lips back and forth and back. I can't seem to make myself stop touching her, and she isn't telling me to stop.

The noise of the bar fades away.

It's just us right now.

"I'm sorry I didn't tell you who I am," I say quietly, leaning closer. "But if you'll let me, I'll show you instead."

There's an obvious hitch to her breath, and she swallows thickly.

I run my thumb over her lip again, her eyes darkening before me.

"Go out with me, Harper. Please."

Another gulp.

Then, a nod.

"Okay."

CHAPTER 14

HARPER

"Be honest. Am I stupid for saying yes to him?"

"Hell no!" Ryan's words echo around my tiny bathroom. I have my phone propped up against a bottle of hair serum so I can talk to her while I get ready. "No, no, no. You were absolutely, one hundred percent right."

I grin down at her. "You're just saying that because you're totally smitten with his teammates."

She lifts a hand, studying the nails she's painting. "I mean, they weren't bad eye candy. Even though that one guy was a complete grump, he was still hot."

I smile at how she calls Rhodes *that one guy* even though she wouldn't shut up about him on our Uber ride home last night.

Last night when I said yes to a date with Collin…again.

I don't know why I did it, and despite what Ryan says —how can I trust her romantic ass anyway?—I'm not so sure it was the best idea.

But…I could understand why he wasn't completely

forthcoming with information the first night we met. I was a stranger and he was in a tough spot. He didn't know if he could trust me.

As for lying the second time, letting me think he was someone else for weeks…well, that part is a little less forgivable.

Even though my brain was yelling at me to tell him no, that's not what my mouth said.

It said yes.

Well, more accurately, it said *okay*.

So here I am, getting ready for a date with an NHL player.

"Wear it down," she instructs as I go to put my hair up in a ponytail.

"What if it gets in the way? I don't even know where we're going."

"He wouldn't tell you?"

"No. And I told him that was incredibly inconvenient for me because I have no idea how to dress, but he just laughed. Laughed, Ryan!"

"Men." She rolls her eyes. "They just don't get it. He'll probably show up in a t-shirt that clings to those stupid muscles of his and jeans that look like they've been painted on."

I drop my hair and lift my brows at her. "Have you been checking out my date?"

"Of course I have. He's hot."

I chuckle. Leave it to Ryan to be honest about ogling Collin.

Not that I blame her. He is hot.

When I saw him at the game last night, the bright lights of the arena illuminating all his features in a way I hadn't seen before…just wow.

He was attractive in the shadows, but beneath the lights? Even with the cut on his lip and the bruise forming on his jaw, he was beautiful.

I run my fingers through my hair, letting my natural curls do their thing. I always save my hair for last, and if I'm wearing it down, then…

I drop my hands to my sides, my palms beginning to sweat as the nerves set in when I realize this is it. I'm going on a date with Collin Wright.

I give myself a once-over. I don't typically wear a ton of makeup, and tonight is no exception. Just a few coats of mascara, a light layer of eyeshadow, and a soft matte pink lipstick. Since I have no clue where we're going, I went with something casual. I paired jeans that hug me in all the right places with a simple burnt-orange tank top, a color block cardigan to match, and a pair of Converse.

"Do I look too…plain?"

"No."

"You're not even looking at me!" I complain.

"Because I don't need to. There is nothing about you that's plain. I promise."

"That sounds almost like both a compliment and an insult."

"Because it was."

I stick my tongue out at her. "Brat."

"You love me. Now, do me a favor and head for the kitchen."

I don't ask what we're doing, I just grab my phone and walk us into the kitchen.

"Get into your liquor cabinet and do a shot of that whiskey you have hidden in the back."

"Ryan! I am not drinking before my date."

"Yes, you are, because I swear I can feel your tension from here. It's palpable."

"It is not," I argue, though I push to my tiptoes and reach for the booze that's stashed away. I pull out a shot glass—one Ryan left here, I'm sure—and pour a drink.

"Quit staring at it and drink it. Here, I'll do one with you."

"You know, it's funny because you sound resigned to help me, but I know doing a few shots is no hardship for you."

"Fine, you caught me. I'm just doing this so I'm not drinking alone."

"I thought you were seeing Steven again tonight."

She sends me a look that says she doesn't want to talk about it and takes a swig from the bottle of tequila she's now holding. I want to press, but I know she'll just change the subject. If she wanted to discuss it, she would. I know her well enough to know when to back off.

"Go on," she encourages. "Drink. It'll help your nerves."

Eh…what the hell. Why not?

I lift the glass and down the hatch it goes, the alcohol burning the back of my throat. I cough a little, shaking my head. "Blech." I stick my tongue out. "It does not mix well with my toothpaste."

"Do another just to wash down the bad taste."

She doesn't have to talk me into it this time.

"Ah. Much better," I say, running my tongue over my lips, already feeling the booze soak into my veins.

"Another?" she asks.

I shake my head. "Better not. Don't want to get drunk on my first date."

"Boo!" She takes two drinks, one for each of us. She grimaces and rubs the back of her hand across her lips, then beams at me, her eyes glassy from the buzz. "I can't believe you're going on a date with an NHL player. Like, what? You hate sports."

"But I love hot men."

She giggles. "Hot men are nice. Especially ones who won't screw you around." She adds the last part quietly, but I know what she's referring to. It's on the tip of my tongue to ask her if I should cancel tonight and spend the evening with her, but I know she'll probably yell at me if I even suggest it.

She shakes her head like she's shaking away bad thoughts. "Anyway, I had better get a text or phone call when you get wherever you're going tonight. Just in case I need to come rescue you."

I look pointedly at the bottle in her hand. If anyone is doing any rescuing tonight, it'll be me rescuing her. I make a mental note to keep my phone close in case she needs me.

"What?" She shrugs. "I'll Uber."

My doorbell sounds and my back goes ramrod straight.

Holy shit! "He's here!"

Ryan's eyes widen and she does a little happy dance. "Ahh! Okay, okay. Go buzz him up. Then bang him. Then go on your date."

"Ryan!"

"At least give the guy a blow job!"

I shake my head, trying to hold in my laughter as I head to the living room to buzz Collin in.

"Fine." She huffs. "Date first, then banging."

"Behave. He's on his way up," I tell her.

"You better keep me on the phone until he gets there. I want to lay down some ground rules."

"No. I'm hanging up now."

"You're no fun." She pouts. "But fine." She seems to sober up for a minute and stares deeply into the phone. "If you need me, call me. No matter where you are. No matter how far."

"Now I really know you're drunk. You're speaking in song lyrics."

"I was quoting a queen, thank you very much. Have fun tonight. For yourself, and me."

"That might be more fun than I can handle."

"Probably."

There's a knock at my door and Ryan squeals loudly.

"Shh!" I hiss.

"Sorry, sorry. I've just never been so excited for someone else to get dicked before."

"Ryan Felicity Bell!"

"What? You know you love me."

"I do. Which is why I'm hanging up."

"You're not moving," she says.

"It's because I'm nervous."

"Don't be. Just go. Be yourself. He's gonna love you as much as I do, I just know it."

"You're my best friend. You have to say that."

"Do not. Love you. Bye."

She hangs up, leaving me standing there staring at my phone, still unable to move.

Another knock sounds at the door, and I jump.

I rub my hands over my jeans, blowing out a heavy breath. Then another.

Okay. It's okay. I can do this. I got this. It's just a first date. I've had those before. It's no big deal. Sure, it's with an NHL player, but whatever. I got this.

"You know you're talking out loud, right?"

I let out a squeak, and Collin's deep rumbly laugh filters through the door.

"I promise not to bite. Well, that's not true. I'll nip at you, but not in places anyone else can see."

If he thinks that's going to help my nerves, he's wrong.

If anything, the way his words have my legs feeling like jelly makes me want to hide even more.

"Harper…"

My name on his lips is my undoing.

I peel the door open and…

Son of a bitch. Ryan was right.

He's wearing a deep green t-shirt that clings to him and a pair of jeans I'm certain look really good from behind. There's a dark brown leather jacket draped over his shoulders that makes him look just a hint dangerous with his split lip. A layer of stubble is covering his jaw and the bruise I know is there too.

When I finally drag my eyes up his body and to his face, I find him staring down at me with a grin.

"Hi."

The word comes out as a whisper, and his grin grows.

"Hi."

His eyes flit over my shoulder, taking in my small, sparse apartment. It's probably not nearly as big and flashy as what he can afford.

"Do you, uh, want to come in for a moment?"

"Actually, we're kind of on a time crunch."

"Are you going to tell me where we're going?"

"No."

A simple answer followed by another grin.

"Okay, but if we get there and I'm not dressed appropriately, I'm going to…to…kick you in the shin."

"Because that's as high as you can reach on me?"

My brows shoot up, and it's not lost on me how I have to tip my head back to look at him properly. "Was that…a short joke?"

"Yeah. Did I need to lean down to say it so you could hear me better?"

I laugh, shaking my head, and reach over to grab my purse from the hook beside the door.

"Has anyone ever told you you're a shithead?" I ask, forcing him out of my doorway as I pull my front door shut and lock it.

"A few times." He's standing close, his warmth flowing over me and making me already wish I'd worn my hair up. His lips graze my ear. "You look gorgeous, Harper."

I gulp. "Thank you."

We make our way to the elevator and take the short ride down four floors in silence. The car is small and usually feels as such, but with Collin in here, it feels even tinier.

He holds the door open for me as we exit the building, his hand landing on my lower back as he steers me in the right direction.

We're not taking a car, and suddenly I'm glad I didn't wear any heels.

We walk side by side for about half a block, not speaking a word, our arms brushing together every few steps.

"So, hockey, huh?"

He barks out a laugh. "That's where you want to start?"

"I mean, it is kind of a big deal for you."

He lifts his broad shoulders. "You could say I'm a

fan."

I narrow my eyes on him. "Funny, you said the same thing the first time I asked if you're into sports."

He winces. "I suppose I did. And I wasn't technically lying. I am a fan."

"And a player."

"And a player," he confirms, shoving his hands into his pockets. "I'm sorry I wasn't honest with you, Harper."

I stop walking, and he comes to an abrupt stop too.

We stand in the middle of the sidewalk, staring at one another.

"I know you are, Collin. But I also want you to know that even if you think you're doing it for the right reason, I won't tolerate being lied to."

He nods once. "Understood."

We resume walking.

"So what's an NHL player doing on a dating app anyway?"

He laughs, but there's no humor to it. "It's stupid, really. I've been…having some trouble this year getting out of my head and into the game. As you can imagine, dating is hard. So I figured…"

"You'd find someone on the app and bang it out of your system?"

He winces. "Shit. That sounds awful, but yeah, pretty much. That was before I saw you on there though. When I came across your profile, plans changed and I—"

"So you don't want to sleep with me?"

"What? No! I mean, yes! Of course I do. You're gorgeous. I would totally sleep with you. I—oh." He takes in the grin on my face. "You were teasing me."

"I was. But it's good to know..." I peek up at him. "Just in case."

His eyes spark with interest at my words. "Just in case, huh?"

"Yeah."

Before I know it, large hands are circling my waist and I'm being pulled into an alleyway and backed up against a wall.

Collin cages me in, one hand on my waist, the other cradling my head so it doesn't bounce against the brick wall. He's holding his body off mine but not so far away that his warmth isn't seeping into my bones.

Yeah, I *definitely* should have worn my hair up. Sweat begins to form on the back of my neck, and it has nothing to do with the weather outside. It's a cool, October evening. Not an ounce of humidity in the air.

His green eyes bore into me as he steps closer. "Just in case what, Harper?"

Just like before, my name rolling off his tongue does something to me.

My knees nearly buckle, but he holds me up with ease.

"I-I thought we were on a time crunch?" I ask, out of breath even though I haven't done anything to cause it.

"We are, but I have time to listen to your just-in-case scenario."

I swallow the lump in my throat, my tongue darting out to wet my dry lips.

His eyes follow the movement. His hand leaves the wall to cup my face, his thumb tracing along my lip just like it did last night.

I hold my breath, relishing the feel of his simple touch that I swear I could still feel as I fell asleep last night.

It was like he'd burned my skin and marked me.

"You smell like whiskey."

"I took some shots."

His brows pinch together in an unasked question.

"I was nervous," I explain. "You make me nervous."

"I do?"

I nod, unable to speak.

He stares at my mouth, watching the thumb he's brushing back and forth.

"I should have kissed you," he murmurs. He drags his eyes back to mine. "That night after our drive…I should have kissed you."

"You should have," I agree. I wanted him to so badly. "I would have let you."

"I want to kiss you now."

"You can."

His eyes darken at my words and he leans in closer, lips hovering just an inch above mine.

"I can't." The words are whispered, and neither of us misses the whimper that leaves me. "If I kiss you now, I won't stop."

"Is that a bad thing?"

"It is when I have a whole evening planned."

"Do we have to go?"

He lets out a string of curse words, then puts some space between us. "Yes. I told you I wanted to show you who I am, and I meant that. I want to earn your kisses, not take them from you."

I want to point out that he's not taking, I'm offering.

But I also respect his desire to want to make up for his mistakes.

"Is this one of those times when you're being a gentleman?"

"Yes. So enjoy it while it lasts."

I grin and push off the wall.

"Then lead the way."

CHAPTER 15

"You can't be serious."

"Oh, I am."

She stares up at the building in question. "This is cruel."

She has no idea what I have planned next.

"It's not."

"But I'm going to want to take them all home."

"You will."

"And I can't take them all home."

"You can't," I agree. "But trust me, this is the next best thing."

"Fine but I swear, if I walk out of here with a broken heart, I want it on record it's your fault."

"Deal."

I pull open the door to Pawever in Love and usher Harper inside.

"Ah, Collin! It's so good to see you. We missed you this summer."

Harper gives me a quizzical look, and I hope the one I send back says *I'll explain later.*

"Hey, Rachelle," I say to the vet tech sitting behind the counter I've stood in front of too many times to count. "How are the kids?"

"They're a handful. You just missed them actually. Dante is starting first grade this year, and Dixon is in sixth. He told me he wants to play football."

"Football? He sure he doesn't want to do hockey instead?"

She laughs. "I told him you'd say that, but..." She shrugs. "He's obsessed with Tom Brady."

"I'll make sure to pop in one day when they're here. Maybe I can sway him." I wink. "What about the other kids? They ready for us?"

"Oh, of course. I'll go grab them." She gives me a warm smile, shaking her head. "You have no idea how much we—and they—appreciate it. We all know you're busy, busy, busy. How you find the time, I don't know, but we don't take it for granted, that's for certain."

"Trust me, I do this for me just as much as I do it for them."

Rachelle scurries down the hall and I turn to Harper, whose stare I can feel burning into the side of my head.

"Do you come here often?"

"Whenever my schedule allows. I usually stop in a few times a week if we're on a home game stretch. Typically I spend a lot of time here in the off-season, but this year Coach thought it would be best if I went back home."

She nods, understanding. "The arrest."

I try not to wince. "Yeah."

"And what do you do here? Volunteer?"

"I—"

The scraping of excited paws on the floor draws my attention, and I turn to find Rachelle being pulled down the hall by two rambunctious pups.

"Ah, Mario, my man!" I drop to my haunches as my favorite English bulldog scrambles over to me, jumping into my lap as best as his stubby legs allow. I rub my hand between his ears as he digs into me, licking at my shirt. "Missed you too, buddy."

A Chihuahua, a new dog I don't know, tries to push Mario away, but he's not budging.

"And what's your name, huh? Please tell me it's Luigi."

"As awesome as that would be, no. This little princess is Nacho."

I glance up at Rachelle. "Nacho?"

"She was found out behind a bar eating nachos and the name stuck."

Much to Mario's dismay, I run my hands over Nacho. She looks to be in good shape. No scars or visible issues. "Nobody claimed her?"

"No, but someone called looking for a Chihuahua not long after she was brought in. When I told them about Nacho, they seemed to be relieved and hung up. I'm guessing she was theirs and they dumped her somewhere, then felt guilty and wanted to make sure she was okay."

"Fuckers," I say. "Sorry for the language."

Rachelle waves her hand. "Please. My husband was in the Marines. He says ten times worse."

I stand and both dogs jump at my shins, not wanting me to let them go. Nacho prances over to Harper, smelling her, then curls up on top of her feet.

"Ah, hell. I'm so rude. Harper, this is Rachelle, my favorite vet tech. Rachelle, this is Harper. She's..."

"A friend," Harper supplies, sticking her hand out to greet Rachelle, who bounces her eyes between the two of us, not buying the *friends* thing for a second. "Lovely to meet you."

"Likewise." Rachelle leans in. "Don't let this man fool you. I know Penny is his favorite. She's about sixty-five and is always patting his ass. We all know she's the reason he keeps coming back."

Harper laughs. "I'll take your word for it."

Rachelle hands Nacho's leash to Harper and Mario's to me.

"All right," she says, "you four have fun. Just make sure they're back within the hour so we have time for cleanup."

"Yes, ma'am," I say, letting Mario pull me toward the door.

We head out the front door and don't even make it twenty feet before someone stops to pet the dogs.

"So, a hockey player with a soft spot for animals,

huh?" Harper asks once we're finally on our way to our destination.

"Yep." I nod. "We had a dog growing up and I loved him so much. We went everywhere together. I swear I cried for about three weeks when Bobby passed."

"You named your dog Bobby?"

"Yep. After Bobby Orr, one of the greatest defensemen to ever play the game."

She grins. "Of course you did."

"Anyway," I say, steering us toward the park not too far up the street, "I've always wanted to get a dog, but since it's just me, and with my schedule, it's not something I feel right doing. So instead, whenever I can, I walk the shelter dogs. That way I get my dog cuddles in and they get the love and attention they deserve."

"That's incredibly sweet, Collin."

"It's really no big deal." I shrug, hoping she doesn't see the heat I feel coating my cheeks.

When we finally reach the park, I lead the dogs over to the sectioned-off area and let them off their leashes inside the fence.

They go nuts, running back and forth and back, stopping to pee every few feet to mark their territory.

We take a seat on the bench, letting them play for a few minutes but keeping an eye on them.

"Can I tell you something?"

I glance over at Harper. Her eyes are trained in the direction of the dogs but her gaze is far away, somewhere else entirely.

"Sure."

"In the car, I had this whole image of you built up in my head. You were this regular guy who worked in the sports industry"—I ignore the pointed look she gives me —"and you did and liked normal things, like fast-food chicken nuggets and horror movies."

"I still like those things."

"Right. But when I found out you're a hockey player, that all got erased. You became…" She lifts a shoulder, shaking her head. "I don't know. Something else. Something…bigger. And now…"

"Now?"

"Now I kind of want to kick you in the shin still."

I tilt my head on a laugh. "Why?"

"Because you're still this big, untouchable thing, but you're also this normal guy who does kind things like take shelter dogs for walks and talks to Rachelle about her kids and saves me from drunken idiots and beats people up because they're awful to your brother. It's annoying."

"Annoying?"

"Yes! Because you're…" She throws her hands in the air like she's exhausted. "Well, *you*! Hot, famous hockey player with a bad rap but a secret heart of gold. And, well, I'm just me."

"First of all," I say, shifting toward her, one arm outstretched on the back of the bench, the other hand going to her face to bring her eyes to mine. "I'm flattered that you think I'm hot."

She rolls her eyes, trying to pull out of my grasp, but I don't let her.

"Second, I'm still me. Aside from not telling you that I play hockey, everything I told you was all true. Hockey is a big part of my life, yes, I won't deny that. But I have an identity outside the game too."

"I know that. I just—"

"Third," I interrupt, "you are not *just* you, Harper. You're smart and funny and gorgeous. Talented as hell. You do that *cute*"—I make sure to emphasize the word—"rambling thing. You like what you like and you don't apologize for it or try to fit into some box for society. You're you…and that's exactly why I like you."

Her eyes are searching mine, looking for any hint that I'm lying, I'm sure.

But I'm not. I mean it.

I know it's so fucking cliche to say the whole *You're not like other girls* thing, but in this case, it's true. If her profile hadn't stuck out because I knew her, it would have for a different reason.

I've lost count of the number of times I've met the wives of my teammates and they start to tell me about themselves and it sounds like they're reading from the same script. Hell, even their social media pages all look the same. Same filters, same content, same sponsored posts, same outfits, same houses.

Same, same, same.

It gets old. It gets boring.

Harper? She's anything but boring.

"And fourth?" I lean closer, and whether she does it on purpose or subconsciously, she does the same. "I assure you, I am *not* untouchable. You can touch me any time you want."

"See? That!" She groans, pulling away. "You can't say things like that."

"Why not?"

"Because it makes me like you!"

"Is that a bad thing?"

"I don't know yet."

It takes us fifteen minutes to leave Nacho and Mario behind because Harper couldn't stop hugging them.

"If you love dogs so much, why don't you get one?" I ask as we leave Pawever in Love and head for the parking garage I left my car in.

"I don't know. I'm not sure I'm ready for that kind of commitment."

"Your profile said something about commitment too," I point out.

"I'm just…cautious is all." She doesn't look at me when she says this and I feel like there's something more there that needs unpacked, but it's really none of my business.

Besides, I'm not looking for serious either. Not right now, anyway.

"I understand. You want to keep it casual and see

what happens?"

"Yes. Is that…is that okay?"

Harper helps keep my mind off of the game, and the fact that she doesn't want strings when I'm not in any position to offer them? Yeah, casual is perfect.

"I can do casual."

"Good, good. Glad we're on the same page." She grins. "So, where are we headed now?"

"Dinner, if you'd like."

"Oh good." She pats her stomach, which I'm pretty sure I heard growl a few minutes ago. "I was hoping you'd say that. I'm starving. Where are we going?"

I grin. "It's a surprise."

"I should have known."

"You just have to keep an open mind and maybe keep those dangerous shin-kickers to yourself."

She narrows her eyes but doesn't say anything as I guide her toward my sleek, dark gray Audi S8. I notice the surprise in her gaze when she sees it, but really it's nothing too extravagant, not compared to what most guys on the team drive.

"What happened to your SUV?"

"It's still in the shop. I'm having it repainted and reupholstered."

"Oh." She eyes the car again. "And here I thought my paid-off Honda was badass," she mutters as I help her in. "I feel underdressed for this."

I laugh. "For riding in my car?"

"Yes."

"For what it's worth, I find your paid-off Honda to be very badass."

"You do?"

"Yes. You worked hard for it, and in my book, that's the very definition of badass."

A smile lights her face as I gently shut the door, then round the car, hopping in behind the wheel.

We make small talk as I navigate the downtown area. And by small talk, I mean Harper mostly just googles my car, telling me all about it. Her excitement is adorable, and by the time I'm pulling into yet another parking garage, she's already planned how much money she needs to make a year to be able to afford one of her own.

If it keeps her smiling like she is now, I'll buy her one today.

But I'm not going to tell her that because I shouldn't be thinking that.

What the hell is wrong with me?

I shake myself from my thoughts and help her from the car. She gives me that same dopey grin. It makes me angry and causes something to flutter in my chest all at the same time.

I ignore both reactions and smile back.

"Keep that grin in place."

She drops it, her beautiful white-blue eyes narrowing. "Why."

It doesn't come out as a question and I just smile brighter, leading her toward our destination.

When we stop in front of a nondescript door, she eyes

me cautiously.

"Why do I get the feeling I do not want to go in there right now?"

"I don't know what you mean."

"Collin…"

"Come on. There's food waiting."

That seems to kick her into gear.

We walk through the doors into the dimly lit building. It's a quiet place that serves a little of everything. Nothing too fancy and nothing too plain.

There's music thumping through the speakers as we're guided toward a table. Our server takes our drink order, then promises to be back shortly.

"What is this place?"

"It's dinner. And a show."

She quirks a brow. "What kind of show?"

"The fun kind."

Her lips form a grim line, and I can't help but laugh.

"Open mind."

The server reappears, drinks in hand.

"All right, what can I get for you to enjoy with tonight's entertainment?" They shimmy their shoulders, the fringe on their cowgirl-inspired shirt shaking.

"I'll have the sampler platter and a basket of fries," Harper tells them. "Then whatever he's having."

"Burger, please. Rare. No veggies. Lots of fries if I could."

"Sure thing, sugars. I'll get that order placed and right out for you. Our entertainment will begin shortly.

Just remember to please keep your hands to yourselves. Tipping is allowed and encouraged." They wink. "Have fun, dears."

"Collin…" Harper starts, staring after our server. "Is this…" She looks over at me. "Did you bring me to a drag show?"

"No. It's karaoke. You know, in case you wanted to grace the stage with that wonderful vocal range of yours."

"You ass!" She laughs. "I knew I shouldn't have told you that story, Fartknocker!"

"Okay, that's just rude." She tosses a sugar packet at me. "Hey, no throwing things!"

"I am *not* singing."

"God, I hope not. I hear it's awful." I grin at her over my beer.

"Are you sure it's *just* karaoke?"

"Pretty sure, yeah. I looked it up this morning."

"But…" She looks around. "Maybe you got the date wrong?"

I follow her eyes. The crowd is filled with old and young people alike. There are people dressed casually, people dressed up, and people…

"Oh. *Oh.*"

It's so obvious now, looking around. How I missed this when we first walked in, I'll never know.

She bursts into laughter. "Oh my gosh. You should see your face right now."

"I thought… I…"

Harper wipes her eyes. "Do you want to leave?"

"What? No. Why would I?"

"Because this"—she waves a hand around—"is definitely not your scene."

"If you think this is my first time around queens, you're wrong."

"Really?"

"My brother runs an LGBTQ+ safe house. They do drag nights all the time. I help out around there whenever I'm home."

Her mouth pops open as she regards me.

"What?" I ask, feeling uncomfortable under her gaze.

"Nothing. You just…surprise me."

"Good or bad surprise?"

"Good. Very good."

"Queens, kings, and human beings!" a loud voice booms over the speakers. "Put your hands together because tonight we are joined by the amazing, the vivacious, the downright looking-so-damn-good-it-should-be-illegal Clitney Spears!"

Harper's mouth drops open. "Did they just say *Clit*ney Spears?"

The lights dim, and all that can be heard is a pair of heels clicking across the stage.

Then the low thrum of a song—presumably something by Britney Spears—begins, and the lights come back on one by one, illuminating the stage. The place goes nuts, screaming and yelling as she begins to sing and dance.

"Oh my gosh," Harper says, not taking her eyes off the performer. "This might be the best night of my life."

I wish I could say the set was good.

I wish I could say I experienced something new.

But the whole night, my focus is solely on the woman sitting across from me.

And how I think maybe…maybe she was what I needed all along.

Harper's laugh fills the otherwise quiet hallway. "And then when she landed on your lap, you about fell out of your chair."

She slaps at her thighs, laughing harder.

Tonight—which was supposed to be dinner and karaoke—did not go as I planned. Not just because of the schedule flub, but because one of the performers fell off the stage and landed on my lap. Her heel came up and scratched me right above my eyes, slicing the skin open and causing the show to be put on pause so I could get bandaged.

I'm sure it's already out there on social media somewhere.

Despite the mishaps of the evening, it was still fun. Mostly because watching Harper enjoy herself so much made me happy.

For the first time in a long time, I forgot all about my troubles surrounding the game.

Harper stops in front of her door and all her giggles fade away. She reaches up, running a finger over the cut on my head.

"You're going to get a lot of questions tomorrow, I'm sure."

"Eh. Let 'em talk."

She drops her hands, and I can see the second the reality of this moment settles across her face.

"Well, this is me."

I tuck my lips together, trying not to laugh at her. "Yes, I do recall that from when I picked you up here a few hours ago."

That uncomfortable silence I'm really beginning to hate settles between us again. She peers up at me, practically wringing her hands in front of her in anticipation of this moment.

She's waiting for me to kiss her.

She *wants* me to kiss her.

"Ah, screw it," she mutters.

She shoves up onto her tiptoes, slips her hands into my hair, and pulls me to her.

Our mouths collide and I'm stunned.

I don't think in my entire life has a woman ever taken the initiative to kiss me first.

I wrench my mouth away from her, and she blinks up at me with wide eyes.

"What the hell are you doing?"

Her mouth pops open, surprised. Embarrassed. "I… I… *Oh god.* I'm sorry. I thought…I—"

I back her into the wall, cutting off her words. She lets out a shriek as I haul her into my arms and her legs lock around my waist like they were made to be there. I hold her up with one arm, the other sliding into her hair, my thumb caressing her cheek. Her blue eyes are big and full of shock, and when I press into her, letting her feel just what she does to me, they widen even more.

"Did you just steal our first kiss from me?"

A grin curls into the corners of her lips. "I was tired of waiting."

I shake my head, lowering my head back to hers until our lips are barely brushing.

"*This* is how that was supposed to go."

I slide my lips over hers, gently at first, tasting her slowly and softly.

Her hands slide up my chest, a low moan passing through her, and I snap.

Gone is the slow and soft. I kiss her hard, my tongue pushing past her lips, and I'm a fucking goner.

She tastes like the sweet wine she was sipping at dinner. It tastes good. *She* tastes good.

I push my hips into her, and another soft moan fills the quiet hallway. Her hips move, seeking the friction I'm providing. We're humping each other like a pair of horny teens, and I don't think I ever want to stop.

I brush my fingers under her shirt, needing to feel if her skin is as soft as it looks. Her hands crash into my hair, pulling me closer and somehow tugging me away all at the same time.

"Collin…" she says against my lips.

I pull away with reluctance, my breaths coming in sharp and fast like I just spent a shift out on the ice, and I'd be hard-fucking-pressed to ever admit it out loud, but this? This is better than anything the ice can give me.

"Come inside."

She doesn't have to ask me twice.

I slip out the keys I feel in her back pocket and push one into the door. By some fucking miracle, it works.

I don't move to carry her inside just yet.

A crinkle forms between her brows as she peeks up at me.

"Are you sure?" I ask her. "Because if we walk into your apartment, there's no turning back. I'm going to fuck you, Harper."

She gasps at my words, eyes darkening with lust.

"First it'll be hard and fast," I continue. "Then it'll be soft and slow. And after that, I won't be done with you. I'll want more."

She gulps, her fingers flexing in my hair.

"So, I'm asking you, are you sure?"

Her teeth bite into her bottom lip like she's thinking it over, and I want to pull it free and suck it into my mouth to soothe away the sting.

But I wait.

She needs to make this decision herself.

Finally, it pops free, and the sweetest word ever leaves her lips.

"Yes."

CHAPTER 16

HARPER

Collin's mouth is on mine before I can even finish saying it.

He pushes open my front door, then slams it closed with his foot, never once taking his lips off mine.

He pushes me against another wall, and all I can think of is how fucking hot his muscles have to look under his shirt as he holds me here. I peel the jacket from his body, needing to feel him.

His hands shove at the cardigan over my shoulders, pushing it away. It barely hits the floor before his fingers are pushing my top up, sliding against my overheated skin.

And then my shirt is gone too.

My legs are wrapped around his waist and all I'm wearing is a pair of jeans and my bra.

Damn am I glad I put a cute one on this morning.

Collin stares down at me, his green eyes taking me in. I can feel every inch they roam over, branding my skin with the fire inside of them.

"Bedroom," he chokes out. "Where's your bedroom?"

With a shaky finger, I point at the hallway behind him.

He releases his hold on me, letting my legs drop to the floor.

I almost wish he hadn't because I can't stand right now, I'm trembling with want so bad.

"Go."

One word.

It's all he says.

So, I do. I go.

I stumble past him, rushing down the hall to my room.

He's right behind me, that warmth of his I'm really starting to like enveloping me like a blanket.

When I reach my bedroom, he flicks the light on, and my heart starts to race.

Lights on? What is he, some kind of maniac?

"I want to see you," he explains, like he knows I'm internally freaking out. His hands circle my waist, tugging me back against him.

I feel his erection digging into my back as he picks up my hair and slides it out of his way. His lips dance across my exposed neck. I don't even realize he's unhooked my bra until the material begins to slip down my arms. I let it fall to the floor, acutely aware that I'm half naked and he's fully dressed.

Normally, I'd be embarrassed to be so exposed in front of someone.

But not with Collin.

Never with Collin.

He cups my breasts, fingers plucking at my hardened nipples.

"I've been wanting to play with these since I saw your profile."

"You have?" It comes out a pant as he nips at my neck, then drags his tongue along it.

"Yes." He leaves one hand on my chest, the other lighting a path down my stomach and into the top of my jeans. His fingers play at the edge of my panties. "In one of your photos, you're dressed up, wearing this hot navy-blue dress, and your tits are pushed up high." Another nip. "Too fucking high. I bet everyone was staring at you that night."

"Marine Corps Ball," I tell him as he slips his hand into my underwear and over my neatly trimmed mound. "Ryan's brother is a Marine."

I don't know why I tell him that. It doesn't matter.

"Harper?"

"Hmm."

It's not a question. It's a pure moan as the pad of his finger grazes my clit.

"Don't talk about other men right now. Not when my hand is on your pussy."

I nod and swallow, trying to keep myself standing as

he draws slow, short circles over my swollen bundle of nerves.

I swear I could come right now just from this gentle touch.

The crazy part is I know it's all Collin and not because I haven't been touched in a long time.

I have no idea how long we stand there, him with one hand on my tit and one between my legs, but my bet is that it's not long. I'm on the edge of coming, and I swear, if Collin just applied a bit more pressure and rubbed just two more circles, I'd explode.

But he doesn't.

He pulls his hand away and I whimper.

He chuckles darkly. "Take your pants off and get on the bed."

I don't waste a single second. I yank my pants down my legs—leaving my underwear on—and crawl onto the bed, lying on my back.

Collin stands at the edge of the mattress, staring down at me with obvious desire in his gaze. He strips his shirt over his head, and those abs I've spent far too much time staring at are finally on display.

Fuck, he looks incredible. All defined muscle and sharp edges like he's been chiseled out of stone.

I don't paint often—and certainly not people—but I have the craziest desire to grab my easel and paintbrush and put this image on a canvas.

One knee lands on the bed, the mattress dipping

under his weight. Slowly, almost too slowly, he makes his way to me.

He fits himself between my legs like that's where he belongs, our bodies molding together like they've been made to fit. His cock is straining against his jeans. The material is rough against my skin but still feels so good as he grinds himself against me.

His lips seal over mine in a searing kiss. I let my hands roam his muscles, running them across his stomach and around to his back, feeling the dips and curves and the delicious hardness of him.

Meanwhile his hands are exploring too. His fingers dancing over my sides, tracing a path of their own. He kisses down my chin, down my neck, and down to my breasts.

He keeps his eyes on mine as he closes his mouth around a puckered nipple, sucking it into his mouth expertly. He grazes his teeth over the sensitive spot, then soothes away the bite with a swirl of his tongue. He gives the same treatment to the other one, back and forth and back again until I'm rubbing my pussy against him, needing something to help relieve the blinding ache between my legs. There's no way he doesn't feel the wet spot I'm leaving behind.

Understanding what I need, he gives my nipples one last taste, then drags his mouth down my body, not stopping until he's between my legs.

He nips at the sensitive parts of my thighs, and I can't

help but think of his promise earlier to do just this thing in places nobody would see.

"Do you like these?"

"What?"

"These underwear…" He grazes a knuckle over me and I groan. "Do you like them?"

"I…yes?" I don't know. I can barely think. I can't even remember what I'm wearing right now.

"Well, that's too bad, isn't it?"

I hear the material rip and a rush of cool air hits my exposed pussy.

Without warning, his tongue is there, pushing into my folds. He gives me several long, playful licks, then sucks my clit into his mouth.

I swear I stop breathing.

My whole body quakes as I come harder and faster than I ever have before.

He doesn't let go. Just keeps licking and sucking at me, draining me. Bringing me right back to the edge like some magician.

Just when I'm about to come again, he pulls his mouth away.

"Oh my god. I hate you."

He laughs, crawling back up my body. "Based on the way your cunt was squeezing my tongue, I highly doubt that."

Cunt.

It sounds so dirty, the way it rolls off his lips and against mine. It's…oh god. It's kind of hot.

He presses his mouth to me and I taste myself on his lips...on his tongue.

I want to cry when he pulls away, but when he pushes off the bed and stands, then flicks open the button of his jeans, I decide it's okay.

He reaches into his back pocket and retrieves his wallet. He grabs a condom from inside—I don't want to think about why he has it on the ready—and tosses it at me.

His hands go to his jeans again and he lifts a brow, waiting.

If he thinks I'm about to stop this, he's wrong.

I want this too damn badly to stop. I want to feel him on top of me...inside of me. I want to watch him fall over the edge just like I did.

When I don't say anything, he slowly pulls the zipper down, and I don't take my eyes off him for a second. Not when he pushes his jeans and underwear off. Not when he crawls back onto the bed, leaning over me on his knees as he peels open the condom. Not when he rolls the rubber down his length, stroking himself a few times as his eyes drift to the exposed place between my legs. And not when he lowers himself on top of me, wrapping a leg around his waist and lining his cock up with my entrance.

It's only when he slowly slips inside of me on a groan that I close my eyes and relish the way he feels as he stretches me more than I've ever been stretched before.

He's big and it hurts, yet it feels so good at the same time.

"Look at me," he instructs.

I do.

"Fucking Christ," he mutters, holding himself off me, not daring to move as I adjust to his size. "You feel amazing. So fucking good. Better than I imagined."

"You imagined this?"

"Too many fucking times."

He gulps once. Twice. And I don't miss the tiny beads of sweat beginning to form at his temples.

"Collin?"

"Yeah?" It's strained sounding, but I hear him.

"I thought you said hard and fast."

His eyes snap to mine at my words, and it's like something in him breaks.

He lets go of all the restraint, going onto his knees, and plows into me with expertise. I try not to think about how much practice he has compared to me, how he's likely honed this skill of his as much as his skill on the ice.

He drops his forehead to mine, pushing into me again and again.

"Only you, Harper," he whispers. "Only you."

I don't know what he means, but I soak in his words all the same.

I run my hands over his back, pulling him closer as he continues to pump into me. I love the way his muscles strain against my hands, the way his body moves on top of mine.

He slides a hand between us, his finger finding my clit, stroking me in those decadent circles again.

My second orgasm hits me out of nowhere and I fall apart around him.

"Fucking beautiful," he says, stroking me once more.

Like he was waiting for me all along, he grabs my hips, pounding into me harder and faster until finally, he stills. His mouth drops open, eyes screwed shut tightly, head thrown back as he comes.

He collapses onto the bed beside me. My hands are shaking as I lie there, completely spent.

The only sound in the apartment is our arduous breathing, and I bet if he tried really hard, Collin could hear the sound of my heart trying to burst out of my chest.

This is just casual, Harper. Nothing to get attached to.

I just have to keep reminding myself of that.

The morning light reaches across the bedroom and into my eyes, pulling me from my dream I really don't want to wake up from.

I dreamt I was in bed with Collin. Dreamt he buried his face between my legs until I came and came. Dreamt he fucked me hard, then slow, then woke me up with his face between my legs again.

I stretch against my blankets, my body sore and tired.

And that's when it hits me.

Last night wasn't a dream.

All those things happened.

Collin.

I peel my eyes open, searching for him, but his side of the bed is cold, like it's been empty for some time.

I sit up, looking around the room for any sign of him. His clothes that were strewn across the floor are gone. The towel he used after a shower—the one he threw on the floor by the dresser—is nowhere to be found.

He's gone.

I try not to let myself be disappointed by that, because of course he's gone. I'm sure staying over after sex doesn't scream casual. Besides, it's not like I expected him to be cooking me breakfast or anything.

He left because I essentially asked him to.

A goodbye would have at least been nice though.

I pull myself out of bed, willing my brain to ignore the aching, and make my way to the bathroom.

I do my business and hop in the shower, trying to wash away how I'm feeling right now.

When I finally make my way into the kitchen, I pause.

Sitting on the table is a bright, baby-blue box. There's a piece of paper next to it.

I feel guilty being upset with him and assuming he left without so much as an afterthought, but more so I'm mad at myself for even caring so much because I know I shouldn't.

I reach for the paper, and a grin covers my face before I even read what it says.

Mornin', gorgeous.

I hope these donuts make up for the fact that I had to bail early. They're from a local food truck. It's one of my favorite places in the city. I'll take you in person next time, if you'll let me. Man, do I hope you'll let me.

Col

P.S. Did you know that you sing in your sleep? Your parents were right to pay you to not try out for American Idol.

I peel open the lid, and sitting inside are two donuts: one glazed and a chocolate one that's drizzled with white icing.

I go for that one first.

I take a bite and nearly moan.

He remembered.

Hidden inside the cake donut is creme filling, and it reminds me exactly of a Ding Dong, only more delicious.

I make a cup of coffee—a combination of salted

caramel and mocha syrup—and take the other donut to sit outside on my patio.

I realize then that I don't have Collin's number, so I pull up the BeeMine app to message him.

HorrorHarper: First, thank you for the donuts. They're amazing.

HorrorHarper: Second, the answer is yes. You can take me in person next time.

HorrorHarper: Third, thank you for last night. It was…wow. I don't even have the words.

HockeyGuy69: I'll gladly take wow.

HorrorHarper: Cocky much?

HockeyGuy69: Confident.

HockeyGuy69: I'm sorry I had to leave early. Morning skate. It's usually optional on game days, but I kind of needed to be here.

HorrorHarper: Totally understand. Though I was a bit worried you had just bailed.

HockeyGuy69: I knew I should have put the donuts on the pillow. But you're kind of a bed hog, and I didn't want you rolling over on them.

HorrorHarper: I appreciate that. I mean, I'd have still eaten them, but thank you.

HockeyGuy69: Someone's already asked about my cut.

HorrorHarper: LOL! What'd you tell them?

HockeyGuy69: The truth. A drag queen beat me up with her shoe.

HockeyGuy69: They won't stop teasing me.

. . .

HorrorHarper: Is it wrong to say I hope it scars? Can you imagine explaining how you got that scar to your future wife and kids?

HockeyGuy69: With any luck, I won't have to.

HockeyGuy69: I already can't wait to see you again.

HockeyGuy69: Can I call you later?

HorrorHarper: I'd like that.

I send him my phone number, and my heart flutters when a text comes through right away.

Collin: In case I didn't make myself clear, last night was WOW for me too, Harper.

Collin: It's gonna be stuck on repeat in my head all day.

Me: For me too.

. . .

Collin: I gotta go. We have some meetings starting.

Collin: Watch my game tonight?

Me: I will.

Collin: See? I knew I'd get you to like hockey.

Me: And all it took was a ding dong…donut.

Collin: *narrows eyes*

Collin: Nothing to do with the orgasms…PLURAL… that I gave you?

Me: I guess they were rather persuasive.

Collin: That's what I thought.

"Ha! I knew it! You're totally going to be a hockey whore now!"

I glare at Ryan from across the table. "Shh! Keep your voice down."

I glance around the sports bar we're at, making sure nobody is paying any attention to us.

When Collin asked me to watch his game and I said yes, I didn't think about the logistics of it. I don't have cable and couldn't tell you what channel to even look for a hockey game on, so I enlisted Ryan's help. She suggested a sports bar.

I think really she just wanted to go out after her night at home nursing her broken heart over Steven.

"I'm not a hockey whore. I don't even know what that is."

"I don't either. I don't know if it's a thing. I just can't believe you of all people are actively seeking out a sport to watch. He must have banged you good last night."

"Ryan!"

"What? He did! I saw the way you limped in here."

I hide my face behind my hands, hoping and praying nobody else is listening in on this embarrassing conversation.

But the truth is…he did bang me good.

So, so good.

Between sleeping in and getting started on my projects late and not being able to think about anything other than Collin's hands on my body, I've been a mess today.

I finally gave up around four and called it a day, soaking in the bath to relieve the stiffness I've been feeling.

"You're awful," I tell her as she peels my hands away.

"And you love it. Besides, if I don't tease you, who will?"

Collin.

"Oh god. You're thinking about him again, aren't you?"

"What? Am not."

"Are too. You're doing that dopey grin thing you do when you think about him."

I give her another murderous glare, and she just laughs.

"So, other than the incredible sex, how was it really? Do you want to see him again...like outside the bedroom?"

That's the thing.

The sex was great, but I think the reason it was so great was because of how good it felt being around him, how easy it was.

I think any other guy I've ever dated would have run the moment they found out they accidentally took their date to a drag show. And they certainly wouldn't have been spending whatever little free time they had at an animal shelter. They wouldn't have held the doors open for me and helped me into their car. They wouldn't have made me laugh until I nearly peed my pants.

With Collin, it feels different.

"It was really good," I tell Ryan. "Almost too good."

"Too good?"

"Yeah. Like you know when you go see a movie and everything about it is perfect. The meet cute, the music, the background stories...you love it all. But then you get home and you read the reviews and see all the little things you missed and it totally ruins the movie for you? That's what it's like with Collin. It's perfect and I'm just waiting for the reviews to roll in to find out that he's not as great as he seems."

"Okay, okay. I hear what you're saying..." She leans her elbows on the table. "But what if it is? What if it is that good and that perfect?"

"That's not possible."

She frowns. "Isn't it though? I mean, look at Goldie Hawn and Kurt Russell. They're not even married and they're thriving."

"They were the exception. And besides, you're just saying that because you're a total hopeless romantic and you're hoping we're going to have some epic love story."

Her lips curve upward. "That's true. I am. But maybe I'm right this time."

"You're not. It's just casual."

"He said that?"

"We both did."

"Hmm. Interesting."

"Why is it so interesting?"

"Nothing," she says, then points to the TV. "Look, your man is back on."

I let her have her not-so-subtle attempt to distract me from our conversation, mostly because I actually do find myself wanting to watch Collin play.

But I don't forget her comment all night long.

Not when the Comets win and Collin calls me after the game, asking to come over.

Not when he strips me out of my clothes and lays me down on the bed, sliding into me slowly.

And not when I fall asleep thinking just maybe…we could be something more.

CHAPTER 17

COLLIN

It's still early in the season and I'm not trying to jinx anything, but we are already on fire. We're on a six-game winning streak, and out of those six games, I've put up a point in all but one.

Coach is happy with me. Shep is happy with me. And Colter is finally off my fucking back.

I don't know if it's just the superstitious hockey player in me, but I can't help but think it's all Harper that has this good mojo flowing.

I think she might be my good luck charm.

"Col, man. That goal was sick. You going out to celebrate?" Rhodes asks, dropping onto the bench next to me. "Hear there are some sick drag clubs here."

We just wrapped up a win in Vegas and we don't leave until tomorrow morning, so some of the guys are going out for a celebratory drink and general debauchery.

I roll my eyes at him. "Nah. I'm good. I'm gonna—"

"Call your girl?"

"She's not *my* girl."

"Dude, come on." He gives me a look. "You call her every night we're on the road, and every night we're not, you're over at her place. Face it—she's your girl."

"No." I shake my head. "It's casual."

That's what we agreed on. Keep it simple and easy. Since my focus needs to be on keeping my numbers up and winning games, I'm perfectly fine with that.

"Uh-huh. Whatever you say."

His tone says he doesn't agree, but he pats me on the back and leaves me to finish undressing anyway.

I hit the showers real quick and change back into my suit just in time to catch the bus. It's a quick ride back to the hotel, and most of the guys drop off their crap and head back out. I stay in, order some dinner, and flop back onto my bed, phone to my ear as I dial Harper.

It's late there, but I know she'll be awake. No matter how many times I tell her she doesn't need to stay up to see the games, especially the ones across time zones, she just laughs.

I don't think she's ready to admit it, but she's totally addicted to hockey.

"Hello?"

"Hey," I say through a grin when her soft, smooth voice hits me. "Please tell me you saw that goal."

"From Colter? Yeah, it was pretty sweet."

A growl vibrates through my chest, and she laughs.

"Yes, Collin, I saw your goal. It was a *beauty*."

"A beauty, huh? Someone has been brushing up on their hockey lingo, I see."

"I might have googled a few things the announcers said. It's like they're speaking a foreign language sometimes."

"You pick up on it fast."

"I'm learning that. So, other than a *beauty* of a goal" —I swear I can hear her smile—"how was your night?"

"Same shit, different city. Just ordered some room service, planning on watching something on TV. But enough about me. How was your day?"

"Long." She sighs, and I imagine she's sitting on her couch, a wineglass in her hand. "But I got three new orders in today, so that makes me and my bank account very happy."

"Am I ever going to get to see your studio?"

"Nope." She pops the P loudly.

Last time I was over there, I tried to go inside to see what it is she does, but she locked the door on me. I don't know why she's so self-conscious about it. Clearly she's talented if she's making a living doing it.

But I'll let her have it for now.

"So, whatcha wearing?"

She barks out a laugh at my sudden change in subject. "Wow. Very subtle."

"That doesn't answer my question."

"No, I guess it doesn't."

I hear water, and I sit up in bed. "Are you in the tub?"

"Maybe." She drags the word out teasingly.

I groan. "You're evil, you know that?"

"You say that like you didn't just see me two nights ago."

"It wasn't enough."

"You just like getting laid regularly."

"And spending time with you."

A knock sounds at my door and I get up, letting the room service in. I give the guy a tip and thank him for bringing it up so late.

When I've settled back onto the bed, I notice that Harper hasn't responded yet.

"You still there?" I ask.

"Yeah."

"You do know it's not just about the sex, right? You know I like spending time with you, yeah? Because in case I haven't said it enough, I like you, Harper."

"I like you too, Collin."

"Enough to show me your titties?"

She laughs. "You just said it wasn't all about the sex."

"And I meant it. But right now, my dick is straining against my pants thinking about you naked in the tub, and I'd really, really like to see your tits."

A beep sounds in my ear, and I pull the phone away.

I grin and hit accept on the incoming FaceTime call.

A bubble-covered Harper fills the screen, and it hits me just how much the words I said before are true.

I like spending time with her, and seeing her now, I miss her.

Not just the sex but *her*.

I'm not used to missing people.

"Hi."

Her cheeks turn pink at the simple word. She props the phone up on something and settles back against the tub. "Hi."

"Anyone ever tell you that you're kind of cute, Harper?"

She rolls her eyes. "Anyone ever tell you that you're kind of annoying?"

"I seem to recall being called that before."

She shifts around in the tub, and the boob gods must be on my side today, because I definitely see nipple.

"Did you just flash me on purpose?"

"Oh. Did I do that?" A wicked grin curves her lips. "My bad."

"You're killing me."

"Am I?"

"Yes. I wish I were there right now."

"I do too."

"How much?"

"So much."

"Can...can we try something?"

She nods slowly.

I scoot back on my bed until my back rests against the headboard. I prop the phone against the lamp and pull my shirt over my head, leaving me in nothing but a pair of jeans.

I settle in on the mattress, picking up the phone and

looking into the camera just in time to see Harper's tongue roll over her bottom lip.

"Are you liking what you see?"

"Yes." There's no hesitation in her answer. "Very much so."

"What would you do if you were here now?"

"I'd probably run my tongue over your abs." The pink on her cheeks deepens. "I've been wanting to do that for a long time now."

"Is that so?" She nods. "I'd let you, ya know. All you have to do is ask."

"I know." The words come out as a whisper.

"Can I see more of you?"

Her eyes darken and she pushes whatever the phone is resting against back until more of her comes into view.

She drags a leg up, spreading her legs, but all of her good parts are still hidden by the bubbles.

She looks gorgeous resting there. The hot water has her skin glistening and her hair is twisted up in a bun, a few strands hanging down, framing her face just right. Right now, she's the epitome of every teenage fantasy I ever had about catching a hot chick in the tub.

"Fuck," I mutter, and she grins. "You look incredible right now. A wet dream come to life."

She drags her fingertips over the tops of her breasts, teasing herself and me.

"Are you wet right now?"

She giggles. "Depends on your definition of wet."

"Your cunt, Harper." She gasps, and just like that, her laughter is gone. "Is your cunt wet for me?"

She swallows audibly and her hand slides over her tits beneath the bubbles, right between her legs.

I know the moment she makes contact with her pussy, her eyelids fluttering shut for only a moment.

"Yes," she mutters.

"Good. Touch yourself. Tell me how you feel."

"Wet." Her teeth sink into her bottom lip as she moves her hand. "Soft."

I slide the zipper of my jeans down, the sound almost deafening in the quiet of the room.

She pauses but I nod at her, encouraging her to keep going as I free myself from my pants.

My cock is throbbing and I want to jerk off so fucking badly, but I refrain.

The water sloshes around her as she continues her ministrations.

"What else, Harper? What else does it feel like? What do your fingers feel like on your pussy?"

"Good," she says quietly. "But not as good as it feels when it's you."

"It is me," I tell her. "I'm there and I'm slipping a finger inside of you."

Her mouth drops open as she does just that.

"I'm sliding it in and out…but slowly. Almost painfully slow, making sure that the edge of my thumb is brushing against your clit with each steady stroke."

She plays with herself, her eyes trying to fall closed

with each pass she makes inside of what is quickly becoming my favorite spot.

"I add another finger, Harper, but I don't pick up my pace."

She adds a second finger, that damned bottom lip of hers being tormented by her teeth again as she stretches herself.

Holy hell, she looks gorgeous. Her head is thrown back as she fights to keep her eyes open with her fingers buried inside herself.

I reach for my leaking cock, swiping my fingers through the pre-cum and using it as lubrication as I begin to lazily jack myself.

I swear she adds another finger without my instruction, and when I ask if she has, all she can do is moan.

Her eyes are closed now, breaths coming in sharp. She's close, and surprisingly, so am I.

"Get there," I tell her. "I'm right behind you."

She slips her other hand into the water, and I know she's rubbing circles on her clit.

I pick up my pace, and just as she begins to cry out, I follow her right over the edge in a sticky mess.

I don't know how long our labored breathing fills the room, but it's long enough that I worry she might have fallen asleep. Her eyes are closed, head resting on the side of the tub.

"You awake still?"

A smile pulls at her lips. "Mmm."

I chuckle. "Get out of the tub before you really fall asleep and drown yourself. I'd rather not have your ghost haunting me forever because I phone-sexed you to death."

"What a way to go though."

Can't argue with that.

"I'm gonna get in the shower," I tell her. "I have…a situation on my hands. Literally."

She wrinkles her nose, still not opening her eyes. "Ew."

"You're telling me. Text me when you get out so I know you didn't drown, okay?"

"I promise."

She looks so sweet lying there all sated and happy.

I wish I were there with her.

I miss you.

It's on the tip of my tongue, but I can't make myself say it because something tells me Harper won't like it.

So instead, I hold it in.

"Good night, Harper."

"Night, Wright."

I hop into the shower, then scarf down my cold pasta from room service.

Just as I'm pulling down the covers to slip into bed, my phone vibrates against the bedside table.

Harper: Don't worry. I didn't drown. Looks like you won't be haunted by the masturbation ghost…for now.

. . .

Harper: P.S. Thank you. I needed that.

Me: Just something to tide you over, you corn dog.

Harper: Did you just call me a corn dog?

Harper: Dammit. Now I want a corn dog.

Me: I meant HORN dog. It autocorrected.

Me: I promise to buy you a corn dog when I get back.

Me: Now go to bed. It's late there.

Harper: Yes, sir.

Harper: OH! *new kink unlocked*

. . .

Me: See? Total corn dog.

"I don't know whether to be completely annoyed or impressed." Ryan's eyes flit between us. "You two did plan this, right?"

"No," we say in unison, which makes this whole situation even funnier.

"Right. Yeah. Totally buying that." She points toward the bar Lowell has set up. "I'll be over there if you two dweebs need me."

Ryan struts over to the bar, sliding up next to Rhodes. He peers down at her. She says something to him, and that frown that's always lining his features deepens, then he stomps away.

Huh.

"You know," Harper says, pulling my attention. "I think she's just mad she understands our costumes."

We weren't lying. We didn't plan it.

But when Harper opened her door dressed as Laurie Strode in a blonde wig, a pair of flared jeans, and a blue button-up complete with a rip in the sleeve, me standing there dressed as Michael Myers felt like fate.

"Probably."

I grab her hand and pull her through the costume party Lowell has been putting on for the team since he became captain. Kids are to be left at home, and drunkenness is encouraged. We try to do it as close to

Halloween as our schedule allows, and it's always a blast
—sometimes probably too much of one even.

I expect tonight to be no different, especially since we
won our seventh game in a row last night.

When we reach a non-crowded spot in the house, I
settle onto an empty chair, pulling her into my lap.

"Got a question for you," I say, peeling off my mask
and running a hand through my hair.

Harper pouts. "You looked cuter before."

"I'm going to pretend you didn't say that."

She rolls her eyes. "What's your question?"

"What did you do with the stick I gave you at the
home opener?"

She sucks in air through her teeth, scrunching up her
face. "Uh...I kind of...gave it away?"

"You did or didn't? Because that sounded like a
question."

"I did." Another wince. "I was mad at you and I
didn't really know what to do with it, so I just handed it
to some kid."

"Did you happen to *look* at the stick at all?"

"I mean, kind of? But not closely. Why?"

"I wrote my phone number on it."

Her eyes widen and she covers her mouth with her
hand. "No."

"Yes. And guess who called me this morning?
Jonathan Lucas Kyler, age 8. He's in Miss McCarthy's
class and he's going to be a defenseman in the NHL one
day."

She laughs. "Stop it."

"Oh, there's more. He prefers cats to dogs—we had a long chat about why he was wrong on that one—and he loves jalapeños on his pizza. He doesn't like ketchup—another blasphemous thing—and his favorite cartoon is *Adventure Time*."

"He sounds a little misguided, but adorable nonetheless."

"We have a training session scheduled for next week. He's offered to teach me a few things that I apparently need help on."

Her shoulders shake. "Oh my gosh. I'm so sorry. I had no idea you wrote your number on it."

I shrug. "It's fine. The kid's a hoot. Maybe he can help teach me a few things."

"Please. You're an amazing player. You don't need any help."

"You should have seen me at the start of the season. I was all out of whack."

"Really? What happened?"

I squeeze her hip. "You did. You're my good luck charm."

"I am not."

"Are too."

She looks like she wants to argue but thinks better of it.

Instead, she looks out at the party, taking it all in.

"I can't believe the captain just opens his home up to everyone like this."

"Oh, he doesn't. This isn't his place. He's just renting it. Lowell is super private. Most of the team doesn't even know where he lives."

"Seriously?"

I nod. "Yeah. He had some...issues before. A relationship gone sour. He really took a step back after everything went down."

"Well, good for him for putting up boundaries. It sucks to be hurt by the people you love."

She sounds like she's speaking from experience and I want to press, but we're interrupted.

"I don't think we've officially met yet," Miller says to Harper. "I'm Grady."

Harper glances at me as if to check to see if he's cool. I nod.

"Nice to meet you, Grady."

"I like your costume. Laurie Strode, right?"

"Yes. Are you a fan?"

"Oh hell yeah. Jamie Lee Curtis was looking hot back then. Hell, she's hot now too. Like in those commercials for that yogurt that makes you shit."

"Helps you shit. Doesn't make you shit," I tell him.

"Eh. Same thing." He takes a sip of what I hope is water because he's not exactly the best at holding his liquor. "Why are you two hiding out over here? I think they're going to set up a game of poker in the basement."

"Does Lowell know that?"

His silence tells me it's a no.

Whatever. I'll let him deal with it. He's the one in charge of all these idiots, not me.

"So, uh, Harper…saw you brought a friend with you."

She rolls her lips together. "I did."

"Is, uh, she single?"

Harper shakes her hand. "Sorta."

"Wanna help a guy out?"

I groan. "Jesus, Miller. You can't ask my date to be your wingman."

"No, it's okay," Harper says. "I'll help you out. If you can find her, tell her you think *Grease* is better than *Grease 2*."

"What's *Grease*?"

"A movie. Don't worry, she'll tell you all about it."

"All right. Thank you."

He takes off excitedly, a new pep in his step.

"You just sent him to the wolves, didn't you?"

"Oh, certainly. Ryan would eat him alive."

"He's a good kid. Hell of a player too. Just a little…"

"Desperate?"

I laugh. "You said it, not me."

"Speaking of desperate…" She leans into me. "I think someone owes me a corn dog."

"Did you just refer to my dick as a corn dog?"

"What? No!" She tosses her head back. "Oh god. That did sound like that, didn't it? I literally meant a corn dog. I am starving and those appetizers are just not doing it. I'm desperate for real food."

I place my hand on her stomach. "I swear this thing is a bottomless pit."

"It really is. And I'm sure all this food will catch up to me one day—and hopefully go straight to my ass—but until then, I'm going to enjoy it and eat until I burst."

"First of all, I think your ass is just perfect." I slip my hand over it, giving it a squeeze. "Second, let's get out of here. There's a place I know that serves fair food all year long."

"Seriously? Like funnel cakes and root beer floats?"

I swipe at the corner of her lip. "You're drooling."

"Shut up." She swats at me. "And lead the way."

She pushes off my lap and pulls at me to get up too. I grab her hand and lead her back through the house the way we came.

There are even more people inside than before, but it's like this every year. What starts as a party for the team and their spouses always turns into a full-blown rager.

Harper tugs on my hand, and I look back at her.

"I need to tell Ryan I'm leaving," she says into my ear so I can hear her over the thumping music. She points toward the corner of the living room where Ryan is sitting, talking animatedly. Miller's next to her, and he looks like he's about to hurl. I'm not sure if it's the alcohol I'm almost positive he was drinking or if it's from Ryan laying into him.

Harper makes her way through the throngs of people and I hang back, crossing my arms over my chest, keeping an eye on her. She looks adorably tiny weaving around the tall players, but what's funny is that I'm not sure any of them would be able to actually handle her.

"Huh."

I turn toward the voice coming from my left.

Lowell's standing there, a red Solo cup lifted to his lips.

"Huh what?" I ask.

"You're smitten."

"Bullshit."

"Oh, no, dude. You are *definitely* smitten," Rhodes backs him up, appearing on my right out of nowhere. "It's all over your face. You're totally into her."

"Of course I'm into her. I wouldn't be here with her if I wasn't."

"Yeah, but you're *really* into her," Lowell says.

"Maybe even in love," Rhodes adds.

Me? In love with Harper?

No. Not a chance.

"It's casual," I say for what feels like the millionth time.

"That's what they all say." Lowell sighs. "Then one day they're madly in love and shopping for a ring."

"Then planning a wedding and picking out names for a baby."

Harper and Ryan put their heads together, and Miller takes his chance to slink away by literally sliding to the floor and crawling from their view.

Neither of the girls notice. They're too busy whispering about something. Harper points my way and

Ryan looks over. She grins, then humps the air repeatedly and says something that makes her friend blush.

Harper looks exasperated and shakes her head, but even from here I can see the hint of desire pulling at her features.

Whatever Ryan said, Harper doesn't think it's a bad idea.

And whatever it is, I don't think it is either.

I cannot wait to get her back to my place and show her just how much I missed her over the last few days. I have half a mind to march over there, toss her over my shoulder, and carry her out of the party right now.

"There's that face again," Lowell comments.

I feel my face pull into a scowl. "I am *not* in love with her."

"Methinks the dick doth protest too much," Rhodes mocks.

"Yes, yes. There has been a disturbance in the Force for sure."

"You two are fuckin' nerds."

They don't disagree with me.

"It's not love," I insist. "We're just fooling around. Nothing serious. It's for the team."

They both lean around me, looking at one another.

Lowell's hand lands on my shoulder. "Right."

"Sure thing there, bud." Rhodes pats my other side.

"I fucking hate you both," I mutter, shaking them off.

The girls make their way back over to me, a soft grin playing at the edges of Harper's lips as they approach.

"Heard you're taking my friend home," Ryan says to me. "You gonna bring her back walking crooked again?"

"Ryan!" Harper chides like I'm sure she's done a hundred times before.

"That's the plan."

"Collin! Oh my god." Harper hides her face in her hands.

"Good. That's what I like to hear." Ryan turns her attention to Lowell. "I heard there's a poker tournament in the basement. Wanna go hustle some chumps with me?"

"Fucking hell. Are they gambling again?"

"Oh, yeah, forgot to tell you," I say to him.

"Shit." He runs a hand down his face. "Last time they did this, a brawl broke out and we ended up with two players injured. I think somebody still owes someone else money too. Coach was pissed."

"So is that a yes on the hustling, then?"

"Eh." Lowell shrugs. "Why not? If they're going to get me in trouble, might as well take their money and make it worth it."

He holds his arm out to her, and she hooks her hand around it.

"Text me all the dirty details," she says to Harper.

Rhodes watches them leave, his perpetual sullen stare even more pronounced as they disappear into the crowd.

"I'm heading out," he announces. "Don't text me the dirty details." Then he rakes his eyes over Harper. "Or maybe do."

I step toward him, snarling in warning.

He laughs, shaking his head as he backs away. "Told you so."

"What'd he tell you?" Harper asks once he's gone.

"It's nothing." I hold my hand out to her. "Come on. I'm suddenly starving too."

The way her eyes flare tells me she knows exactly what I mean.

CHAPTER 18

I was right about Collin's apartment being swanky.

We're still in the lobby, but just from the decor and marble flooring, I can already tell whatever awaits us is going to blow my mind.

"Evening, Mr. Wright."

"Hey, Beau. How goes it?"

"Doing well, sir. I see you have a guest this evening." The old man bounces his brows suggestively, and I have a hard time holding back my laugh. "Quite a beauty, too."

I'm suddenly glad we decided to change out of our costumes before grabbing food. Since Halloween was several days ago, we decided not scaring everyone would be best, especially with how recognizable Collin is.

"Are you hitting on my girl, Beau?"

He grabs his chest. "I wouldn't dare, sir." He throws a wink my way. "Besides, Meghan would likely hold a pillow over my head if I even thought about stepping out."

"Oh, she definitely would." Collin waves a hand

between me and the old man. "Harper, meet Beau. He may look old, but he's a spry fella."

Beau sticks his chest out proudly. "That's right I am."

I grin, sticking my hand out. "Pleasure to meet you, Beau."

He grabs my hand in his old, wrinkled one and brings it to his lips. "I assure you, the pleasure is all mine."

"I'm telling you, I got Meghan on speed dial."

"Oh, all right." Beau sighs, dropping my hand. "I get it, I get it."

I smile at their banter, loving their playfulness.

Something I've noticed about Collin is that he takes the time to get to know everyone he talks to. He learns their names and asks them questions. He doesn't brush anyone off like they are beneath him just because he's a famous hockey player.

It's...sweet.

"Here." Collin hands him an Oatmeal Creme Pie he picked up at Fair Foods. "Keep those paws off my gal and there will be more where those came from."

Beau looks at the pie, then at me. "I'm sorry, dear, but this is my first love. My heart belongs to Miss Little Debbie. And Meghan!" he adds. "Her too."

I laugh. "That's all right. Collin here is about all I can handle anyway."

Beau leans in close. "He's quite the shithead, huh?"

"Speed dial, Beau. Speed dial."

The old man sends me a wink, then presses the button for our elevator.

We step in, and even this space is extravagant, smooth, relaxing jazz playing over the speakers.

We don't speak on the ride to the twentieth floor—which is surprisingly fast—and I think it's because we're both too keyed up over what's to come.

When Collin slides his keycard—because a regular key is just too plain apparently—into the door, my knees begin to shake.

I have no idea why. It's not like we haven't done this before.

But there's something different about tonight.

Something that feels more...real.

I don't know if it's because we spent the evening with his team or what, but there's definitely been some sort of shift between us since we left the party.

It makes me uneasy in both a good and bad way.

Good because there's a small part of me that wouldn't mind more with Collin.

Bad because...well, I'm terrified of giving him more. More will only lead to heartbreak. I'm sure of it.

He pushes open the door and a light kicks on the moment Collin steps into the darkened doorway.

"All the lights are automatic," he explains.

I try to rein in my shock but apparently fail as he laughs.

"I came from a three-bedroom farmhouse that was built pre-plumbing. Believe me, I was shocked too when the real estate agent showed me this place."

I step into the hallway, and the first thing I notice is there's nothing in it.

Not a shoe rack or a closet. There's nothing.

"Come on," Collin encourages, motioning with his head.

I follow behind him as he leads me farther into the apartment.

When we reach the end of the hall, everything opens up. What few walls there are have been painted a light gray, and the theme is minimalism.

The first thing I notice is the size. I swear you could fit two of my apartments just inside this space.

The craziest part is there's a whole other level.

The second thing I notice? The windows. They're tall, taking up most of the perimeter. I walk toward them, looking out. We're high up, and with the clear sky tonight, it feels like we're floating.

"I'm still me," he reminds me, coming up behind me.

"This view...it's breathtaking."

"Yes, it is."

But I can see in the reflection that he's not looking out at the night sky at all.

He's looking at me.

His hands come to rest on my waist, and he tugs me back against him.

"It's too bad you took your costume off," I say, leaning into him.

"Why's that?"

"Because I could have made an *Is that a knife you're holding or are you just happy to see me* joke."

He chuckles, grinding his erection against my ass, burying his face in my hair. "Oh, I am very happy to see you. I can assure you of that."

"So it seems."

I try to turn in his arms, but he doesn't let me.

Instead, he crowds me against the cold window, runs his hands along the length of my arms, and picks them up, resting my palms against the glass.

"Keep them there." He drags his fingertips back over my arms and down my sides until he hits my waist again. Slowly, he inches the fabric up, bunching it in his hands. "I'm so fucking glad you brought a dress."

I packed it to wear tomorrow, but it ended up coming in handy tonight. Right now, with Collin's hands sliding the fabric up my body, I'm not mad about that at all.

Cool air rushes against me, my dress now completely gathered at my hips.

His fingers hook into my panties.

"Don't you dare rip them."

A low, rumbly laugh leaves him. "Yes, ma'am." He dips his lips to my ear. "Oh. New kink unlocked."

A laugh bubbles out of me, but it quickly transforms into a moan when he nips at that spot just below my ear.

"I love the way you taste." Another bite. A lick. His fingers tighten on my hips, digging into me, almost bruising.

He drops to his knees, dragging the lace panties down my legs until I step out of them.

I have no idea what he does with them, and I don't care. Not when his hands are on me, pulling me closer until my back is arched, my cheek still pressed against the window.

He shoves my dress back around my waist, leaving me exposed to him completely.

"Hold your dress up," he instructs, and I listen, grasping the material in one hand. His hands roam over my bottom, a single finger tracing down the middle. "Beautiful."

He places a gentle kiss against my lower back as he reaches around, his finger finding my clit.

I suck in a sharp breath at the contact. I'm already teetering on the edge of hanging on.

He kisses me again. Then another and another. Lower, more brazen as he continues to rub circles against my very swollen nub.

Suddenly he stands, and the sounds of him undoing his pants fill the air.

He doesn't once take his finger off my clit, not even when he pushes the blunt head of his cock against me. He's careful not to push into me because we're both aware he's not wearing a condom, but suddenly I *need* to feel him bare.

I push against him, an invitation.

"Please."

I don't have to tell him twice.

He thrusts into me like we have all the time in the world—slowly and softly, relishing the way it feels to have him be inside me with nothing between us.

Once he's buried to the hilt, he begins to pump into me in short, slow strokes.

The roughness of his jeans brushing against my legs feels like a whole different sensation. It feels naughty to be fucking fully clothed.

"Too good." He gathers my loose hair in his free hand, pulling it just tight enough that it stings. "Just too fucking good."

His lips find my neck and he trails kisses all over me, still sliding slowly into me.

"I could get used to this," he murmurs into my ear.

Me too.

So used to it that it scares me. Makes my heart ache with yearning.

But I don't tell him that.

I can't.

I squeeze my eyes shut tightly, blocking out the thoughts as he adds another finger to my clit, his touch growing firmer, just like his strokes.

Our breaths are coming in sharp, the window fogging up with the heat coming from our bodies.

We're both close.

When he abandons my hair in favor of pressing his thumb against my asshole, everything that's been building inside of me breaks and I come with a force I've never experienced before.

Collin pulls out, grabbing my hips and spilling himself across my lower back, like he's claiming me.

He drops his forehead between my shoulder blades as we take in labored breaths, his fingers flexing and relaxing on my hips over and over again.

"You're a beautiful woman, Harper," he says quietly. "But you're even more stunning after I've marked you."

He spins me in his arms and crashes his mouth to mine.

I don't know how long we stand there kissing, but at some point he sweeps me into his arms, carrying me into the shower…where we do it all over again.

After morning skate—because the Comets have a game tonight—Collin lures me out of his bed with the promise of donuts.

When we arrive at the hidden gem—Scout's Sweets —my eyes nearly pop out of my head at the line. It's at least ten deep. At noon.

The food truck is painted a bright blue, matching the box of donuts Collin brought me. There are a few tables set up outside and a small bookshelf to the left of the truck. It's cute and inviting.

"Holy crap," I whisper. "This is insane."

"It is, but it's so worth it."

"We don't have to wait in this line," I tell him. "We can just go to Dee Dee's or something."

He cuts a sharp look my way. "Bite your tongue, woman."

I'm about to make a snarky, inappropriate comment when a young kid comes strolling up to us.

"Hey, mister," he says, pulling on Collin's jacket, tipping his little head back to look at him. "You're that hockey guy ain'tcha?"

Collin grins. "Depends. Are you a Comets fan?"

The little kid puffs his chest out. "Sure am."

"Oh my gosh," says a woman a few people in front of us, turning to look. When she spots the kid standing by Collin, she darts our way. Collin holds his hand up to her, letting her know it's fine.

"Then, yeah, I'm that hockey guy." He crouches down until he's eye level with the little munchkin who can't be more than five. "Collin Wright is the name. What's yours?"

"Jefferson."

"Jefferson, huh?"

"Yup." He bobs his head. "But all my friends call me Jeff. Since my mama said you and I can't be friends, I guess you gotta call me Jefferson."

"I can't be your friend? Why not?"

He hooks his thumbs into his belt loops and kicks at the rocks on the ground. "She said you're too famous and you ain't got no time for bad kids like me who don't clean their rooms."

Collin looks up at the sky, trying not to laugh at the poor kid. "Well, I tell you what, if you pinky-promise me that you'll clean your room today when you get home, I'll be your friend. Heck, I'll be your *best* friend even."

Jefferson's eyes light up. "Really? Oh, man. Petey is gonna be so jealous you're my best friend and not him anymore. He's dumb anyway. He stole my gum. Can you believe that?"

"Kids, man."

"Yeah, kids, man," Jefferson echoes, then he hooks pinkies with Collin.

A few other people in line take notice of their exchange, and it doesn't take long for a line for him to form too.

He stays cool about it, signing whatever they put in front of him, making polite conversation, answering their questions.

When we finally make it to the front of the line, I can tell he's tired and in desperate need of his pre-game nap.

"Hey, Scout," he says to the woman in the food truck with familiarity.

She gives him a shy smile. "Hey, Col. You want your usual?"

"Please, and whatever Harper here wants."

The woman looks over at me and I expect to see jealousy in her eyes, but there's nothing except warmth.

"Hi." She waves. "I'm Scout. It's great to meet you."

"Likewise. I've been dying to tell you that your donuts are amazing ever since Collin brought them to my place."

"He brought you my donuts?" Surprise laces her

voice. I nod and her eyes shift over to Collin, who gives her a bored expression that I'm not buying.

"What?" He shrugs. "It's not a big deal."

"Uh-huh." She punches a few buttons on the screen, muttering something I can't quite make out. "What can I get you?"

"I'll take two Ding-a-ling Dongs and a large iced coffee."

"Sure. Do you want to add any syrups?"

"Do you have lavender?"

"Oh." Scout clutches her chest. "A girl after my own heart." She looks pointedly at Collin. "I like her."

"Yeah, join the club," he says, and I don't miss the smile tugging at his lips.

"If that's all, it'll be eight dollars and seventy-five cents. Want it on your tab?"

Collin nods. "Please."

"Sure thing. Give me a few minutes and I'll bring it out."

We head over to one of the few empty tables, and Collin slides in next to me instead of across from me.

"So you have a tab here, huh?"

"Don't tell my nutritionist, but yeah."

"Your secret is safe with me."

"Keep it that way, yeah? Because I don't want the other guys finding out about this place and ruining it for me, you know?"

I zip my lips together and throw away the key.

He presses a kiss to my temple. "And that's why I like you."

"Oh, is that why you like me?"

Heat flashes in his eyes. "Among other reasons." He brushes his lips against my ear. "Ones I'll tell you about in great detail later."

I shiver at his promise, and he laughs.

Another group of young kids catch his attention and I wave him off, letting him know I'll be fine on my own.

I watch him interact with each person like they're special and have all of his undivided attention. It's remarkable, really. I have no idea how he's doing it.

I'm tired for him.

"He's good with them, huh? He gets bombarded a lot when he comes, and at first, I expected him to just stop showing up, but he never did," Scout says, setting our box of donuts and our coffees on the table. "I put some creamer and sugar packets in the box too. I wasn't sure if you'd need them or not."

"Thank you. I appreciate it."

"Of course." She slides into the spot across from me. "So, how long have you and Collin been seeing each other?"

"Uh…"

She waves her hands. "No, you know what—it's totally none of my business. I'm just nosy and like to keep up with my regulars. None of the other guys on the team have mentioned you, so I was just curious."

"Other players come here?"

"Oh, yeah. Several of them do. And for some reason, they all seem to think they're the only ones who know about this place. It's hilarious to watch them try to tiptoe around one another."

"Men are so clueless sometimes."

She snorts like she knows what I'm talking about a little too well. "Amen to that."

"Your question wasn't invasive, by the way. I... Well, the timeline of things is a little complicated."

"How so?"

I give her a brief history of how we originally met, then found each other on the app and once again at the hockey game. By the end of it, she's shaking her head, pursing her lips in disbelief.

"I should withhold donuts from him. What a total moron."

"Oh, completely. I was furious at first." I glance over at him. He's currently sitting on the ground, his legs stretched out in front of him, showing the kids something. They're all doing exactly what he's doing. "But..." I lift a shoulder. "Here I am."

"I think it's sweet you two fell in love like that. I—oh!" She sits back. "Wow. Your face just totally changed when I said that. I'm sorry. I overstepped again."

I give her a small smile. "It's fine."

We haven't really talked more about what we're doing. There are moments when it doesn't feel at all casual, like something else has blossomed between us and we skipped right over that.

But any time those feelings begin to creep in, I remind myself that we're just having fun.

Collin has a career to worry about, and I'm not looking for serious. It's the perfect scenario, really.

She opens her mouth, then slams her lips back together, rolling them in. "Eh. Who needs labels anyway? You two are adorable together no matter what."

"Thank you."

"I should get back. I have a bunch of things to do before closing up for the day." She stands. "I hope you love the donuts. Feel free to tell all your friends about them."

"Oh, I definitely will."

She goes to walk away, then spins toward me again. "Can I say something else that might be a wee bit over the line?"

"Sure."

"Collin doesn't bring anyone else here. Like, literally *nobody* else. When his family was in town last time, he didn't even bring them. So, take that however you want."

That…surprises me.

And I'm also not sure what that means.

Out of all people, why me?

Scout gives me a soft smile. "Hopefully I'll see you around, Harper."

"You will," I promise.

She heads back inside her truck and I graze on my breakfast, watching Collin continue to talk to person after person. I swear, they have to be calling their friends in at this point, but he's taking it all in stride with the patience of a saint.

Like he can feel my eyes on him, he peeks over at me and winks.

That same longing feeling from last night returns.

I could get used to this, he said.

And the scariest part of all?

I could get used to it too.

CHAPTER 19

A puck goes soaring down the ice, just out of reach of Rhodes' blade, and Colorado has iced it. They've been playing this game with us for the last five minutes, flipping it down the ice any time it comes near them over and over again, running out the clock.

We're behind by a point, but there's still enough time on the clock to score again. We know it, and so does Colorado.

Eye contact is made between the players on the ice, and the message is clear: Don't try anything fancy. Don't try to be the hero. Throw everything we got at the net.

And that's what we do.

Except an errant pass skips over a blade and then Colorado has possession and they're flying down the ice…right toward our empty net.

And just like that, our winning streak comes to an end.

With our heads hung low, we skate off the ice,

heading to the dressing room coated in the stench of sweat and defeat.

We were only one win away from beating a franchise record, so this one stings harder than usual.

So, so close.

"We went out there and gave them hell. Be proud of that."

Coach's eyes scan the room, landing on each of us for a solid moment before moving on to the next.

"It's behind us. There's nothing we can change now. We're moving on." He claps his hands together. "Let's get on the bus. Get home and get rested. Got it?"

We all give some form of verbal affirmation and get our asses into gear.

"Hey, man," Rhodes says from beside me, stripping off his pads. "That was a sick pass to Miller."

"Yeah, too bad Colorado picked it off and scored on it."

"That's on the kid, not you. He should have been there."

I shrug.

He can say that all he wants, but we both know it's not true.

It was a dangerous pass, a total risk. And the reward was just not there.

It's the middle of November and we're doing fine in the standings, holding third place with no problem. But I know if we don't keep our momentum up, we'll slide right to the bottom in no time.

I don't want to be at the bottom. I want to help carry my team to the top, all the way to the Finals. And this time? I want to fucking win.

"We're just tired, man. Been on the road too long. We have a solid stretch of home games, and we always play better on our ice."

"Yeah, sure."

He's right about part of that. We are tired. We've been on the road for almost ten days now, one of our longest stretches of the season. The hotel life isn't the worst thing ever, but it does get old after a while. Wears you down.

I am more than ready to be back in my own bed again…and have a certain someone in there with me.

The dressing room is quiet as we shower, gather our gear, and throw our suits back on for the bus ride to the airport. Sometimes we wait until the next morning to fly back home, but tonight, after being away for so long, we're all eager to get back, so we board our flight immediately after the game.

It's late—or early, depending on how you look at it—when we land back on the East Coast.

I'm fucking beat. Bone-ass tired. I don't hang around to chat and hop right in my car, taking off for home so I can get some sleep.

Except I pull into Harper's apartment complex, and it's only then that I realize what I've done.

I meant to drive home, and I drove to her.

For a long time, I sit in my car trying to figure out just what the hell that means.

It's not casual, that's for damn sure.

And it's not love because there is no way Lowell and Rhodes are right. I'm not in love with her.

I can't be. For so many reasons.

This thing we're doing is just supposed to be something to keep my mind off the game. It's supposed to be fun and easy, no strings. Just relieving tension. It's for the team.

Besides, if this did mean something—which it doesn't —I can't invest in someone else right now, not when I don't know if I'll be here next season or not.

But…I meant to drive home, and I drove to her.

I swallow down that hard truth, and when the clock hits 3 AM, I have a sinking feeling in my gut that maybe…just maybe…Lowell and Rhodes were right.

I think I'm in love with Harper.

I'm dressed in a suit every playing day of my life, so I never feel like they're special attire anymore.

But standing in front of Harper, her jaw dropped and pure, unfiltered lust in her eyes? Yeah, I'm feeling really damn good right about now.

I smirk down at her. "I told you."

"Huh?" She slowly—and I mean *slowly*—drags her eyes up my body and back to mine.

"That I look good in a suit. I told you so."

Her tongue slides across her bottom lip as she lets her eyes roam once again. "Yes, you did."

"Why do I feel like you're about two seconds away from hauling me into your apartment and having your way with me?"

She quirks a brow. "Would you complain if I did?"

"Hell no." She lunges for me, and I sidestep her libido-driven reach. "But Ryan might."

"Who?" she feigns.

"Best friend. About yay big." I hold my hand up about where Ryan comes to on me. "Fiery and slightly terrifying. AKA, the woman I am definitely *not* going to double-cross."

Harper tosses her head back, whining. "Do we have to go? I hate peopling."

"Yes. We have to go."

"But…sex." She pouts.

"I thought it wasn't all about sex."

"You said that, not me. I'm just here for the sex."

I brush off the sting of her words.

"Come on. Let's go support your friend."

I pull her out the door, waiting while she locks it, then guide her to the elevator. When we step in, she peeks up at me.

"You know I was just teasing about the sex thing, right?"

I'm not so sure. "I know."

"Good. Because I do like you, Collin. I like what we

have. It's fun and there are no expectations. Things are good like this."

They could be better.

We could be better.

I'm in love with you.

But I don't say any of that.

Instead, I tug her close to me and cover her mouth with my own, hoping my kiss does the talking for me.

"Okay, so explain it to me again."

We're standing in front of Ryan's interactive project.

There's a fancy camera set up in front of a plain white background. Ryan is currently behind the camera, shooting the couple standing before her.

Harper leans over, pointing a finger at the pair currently in front of the camera. "See the headphones? You record something in that booth over there, a message to one another. Something funny, something sweet, whatever you want. Then, you stand in front of the camera and listen to them. Ryan will give them a signal of when she's going to turn it on, and then she just lets the camera capture their reaction. I think her final plan is to take stills from the footage and print them."

"Huh," I say. "So it's just capturing your reaction to hearing something?"

She nods. "Yes, your initial one. It can say so much

about a person, you know. I bet the photos are going to be stunning."

"You artsy people are weird."

She glowers up at me playfully.

"You know we have to do it, right?"

"Really? You want to be part of this human experiment?"

"Sure." I shrug. "Why the hell not? Besides, I'd love nothing more than a photograph of your face when I've said something dirty. I'd hang that right in my living room."

"You don't have any photos in your living room."

"Not yet." I wink.

"Do you really want to do it?"

"Yes, I really want to."

"All right. I'll tell Ryan."

The long, deep green dress she's wearing that clings to her curves until about her knees and then flares out swishes against my leg as she walks away.

She says something to Ryan, who claps her hands excitedly, then waves me over.

"Oh my gosh," she squeals when I approach. "I am so excited you guys are doing this! I mean, I was going to force you to do it anyway, but I am thrilled you're volunteering." She shimmies her shoulders. "All right. So what you need to do is just go into the booths and record a message. It can be as short or as long as you'd like. When you're done, just flip the light switch, and I'll come get you when I'm ready. You'll just stand here and listen and I'll capture it all. Then you'll go back into the booth while the other one goes. Sound good?"

"Easy enough."

Ryan leads us over to the booths. We each take a room, and when the door clicks shut behind me, there's silence.

It's totally soundproof in here. I can't hear a thing from the showing outside.

Sitting in the middle of the room is a stool and a tape recorder. There's a notecard with basic instructions, and that's it.

Nothing else.

I pick up the recorder and sit, waiting for something to hit me.

A few things run through my mind, especially dirty ones because I wasn't joking about wanting photographic proof of the way her eyes light up when I say something inappropriate.

But nothing sounds good enough. Nothing sounds right.

So I close my eyes, relax my shoulders, and clear my mind. It's the same thing I do before every game. I take a moment to breathe, to center myself.

It takes several seconds to get my head right, and when I do, I lift the recorder to my mouth and speak from the heart.

"Okay, are you ready?" Ryan asks, her voice muffled but audible through the noise-canceling headphones.

I give her a thumbs-up.

"All right." She holds up three fingers. "Three... two...one."

She hits the play button, and for a long time, nothing happens.

It's silence.

But if I hold my breath and listen closely, I can faintly hear the soft rustling of Harper's dress as she settles onto the stool.

She must have hit record as she picked it up.

"What the hell am I going to say?"

Her voice comes over the headphones in a whisper, and it's clear she has no clue she's recording.

"Ugh, I can only imagine what he said. It's probably *cunt*. Oh, man. I kind of hope he says *cunt*. That word really does something to me."

I chuckle.

"But no," she continues. "He's probably saying something great. Something epic. Because that's just who he is. He's perfect."

She groans, her voice growing louder. I think she's dropped her head into her hand, her mouth closer to the microphone now.

"Ugh. Why does he have to be so perfect? Why? All the perfect ones end up being the biggest heartbreakers. I should know. My father was perfect too. The best dad, the best husband. But none of that mattered because in the end, he was nothing but a lying, cheating jerk who broke my mother's heart in the worst kind of way. I mean, what asshole goes out for a piece of ass in the middle of a snowstorm and gets himself dead? My father, that's who."

There's a crackling as she readjusts herself.

"But god…the way he looks at me sometimes. It's like he's peeking into my soul. Like he sees *me* in all my awkward glory and actually likes it. Likes me. It…it feels so good to be wanted like that."

She sighs heavily.

"I think I upset him earlier when I told him it was just sex for me. It was a lie. It's not just sex, and it scares me so much. It scares me because I think maybe he might be falling for me and I…I can't. I can't fall for him. I can't put myself out there like that. I can't let him be the second man to break my heart. He's… It's not worth it."

She exhales sharply.

"Okay, Harper. You can do this. Just say something fun. Tell him he has a cute ass or something. Yeah, that's what I'll go with."

Not realizing she was already recording, the air goes dead when she clicks the button.

I don't move.

I can't.

I thought the worst moment of my life was when the lamp lit up in overtime in Game Six.

But no.

This is it.

Because the girl I'm in love with? The one I just confessed my feelings to on that recording she's just minutes away from hearing?

She just told me I'm not worth it.

CHAPTER 20

HARPER

The tension in the car is thick. Like suffocatingly so.

When I listened to Collin's message, I wanted nothing more than for a Hellmouth to open up beneath me and swallow me whole. There would be no badass Slayer coming in and saving the day either.

I'd deserve all the pain and the punishment.

Because I told him his ass was nice.

I fucking told him his ass was nice!

And what did he say to me?

It doesn't matter. It doesn't matter because all I could think to say was something stupid, and every word he uttered in that deep, seductive voice of his was the opposite of that.

It was perfect.

It made my heart race. Made my fingertips tingle.

It made me feel alive.

And I screwed it all up.

"Col—"

"I think we should stop seeing each other."

Those eight words feel like a thousand tiny razorblades slicing into my skin all at once.

But…I think he's right. I think we should stop seeing each other too. Because clearly we're not on the same page.

I think he has a nice ass, and him? He…

I can't say it. I can't even think it.

It hurts too much.

"Okay."

"Okay," he echoes, pulling into my apartment complex.

He pushes the gearshift into park and shuts off the car. He opens his door and rounds the front of the vehicle to mine.

Of course he's going to walk me.

Of course he's going to be a damn gentleman.

He pops open my door and holds his hand out for me.

Reflexively, I slide my palm against his, letting him help me out. I don't bother acknowledging the tingles making their way through my body.

He clicks the key fob to lock his car, then rests his hand on my lower back, guiding me into the building.

We don't speak as we step into the old, cramped elevator.

When we get to my door and I push the key into the hole, we're quiet.

Even when Collin follows me inside and down the hallway to my bedroom, it's silence.

When he peels my dress from my body and buries himself inside of me…nothing.

This is our goodbye.

He knows it and so do I.

We don't try to ruin it with words.

In the morning when I wake up to a cold, empty bed, that's when tears come.

I held him at arm's length. Refused to let him in for fear of getting my heart broken.

I was a fool to think he wouldn't break it anyway.

CHAPTER 21

COLLIN

"I fucking swear, Colter, if you get in my lane one more time, I'm flattening your ass."

"Oh, fuck off, Wright." He skates right up to my face. "You've been screwing up all morning. This isn't me." He shoves at me. "It's *you*."

I shove him back. "Bullshit it is. You can't keep your shit straight, shooting pucks all over the ice like some rookie."

"Hey!" Miller protests.

We ignore him.

"Some of us are over here trying to fix shit."

"I bet it's your fault," Colter sneers, "this losing streak we're on. You fucked it up, didn't you?" He presses his nose to mine. "What happened? Your little piece of tail run off on you? No more good luck charm for you. You didn't fuck her good enough, did you?" He laughs. "You should have sent her my way. I'd have taken care of her."

For the second time this season, I attack my own teammate.

Only this time, he doesn't get a lick in at all.

I rain blow after blow down on him, hitting him for all the times he's pissed me off in the past. My knuckles are starting to hurt, and I don't even care. The bite feels good because anything is better than the way I'm feeling right now.

An arm wraps around my waist and hauls me off of my downed teammate. He's bloody and swollen and I don't even give a shit.

"Don't fucking talk about her! Don't go near her!" I yell as Lowell drags me off the ice. "You fucking hear me, Colter?"

"That's enough," Lowell says lowly into my ear. "You're done."

He doesn't let me go until we're off the ice and down the tunnel.

"Fucking shit," he says to my back as he follows me into the dressing room.

I crash onto the bench, putting my head in my hands, trying to hide how much they're shaking.

"What the hell was that, Col? You were relentless."

"Yeah, well, the dude has been on my ass all season." I sit back, sucking in a breath, trying to calm my racing heart rate. "I'm tired of it."

"No. *You* instigated it this time. There's more to it than that." Lowell stands over me with his hands on his hips. "What's going on, dude?"

What's going on?

What's going on is that I'm fucking miserable.

I haven't seen or talked to Harper in a week. I can barely sleep, my stomach is all tied up in knots, and any time I do anything to try to get my mind off shit, it's pointless because it always somehow comes back to *her*.

I feel like I'm back where I was at the beginning of the season, the weight of everything crushing me, pulling the air from my lungs and suffocating me.

The worst part is that it's my own stupid fault again.

But I don't tell him all that.

In fact, I don't say anything at all.

He takes a seat next to me, sighing. "Is what Colter said true? Did you and Harper break up?"

"We were never together."

He lifts a brow. "Certainly seemed that way to me."

Yeah, me too.

"Nope."

He just nods. "All right. I'll let you sell that story if you want." He scrubs a hand over his face. "Fuck, man. You really laid into him."

"He had it coming."

Lowell's lips twitch. "Maybe."

The dressing room door slams open and I inwardly groan as Coach comes barreling in.

"You." He points at me, his finger shaking, probably from anger. It's radiating off him like he's fucking Godzilla all charged up and ready to blast. "You're benched."

"What?!"

"Boy!" He stalks across the floor, getting right into my face. "That circus out there was bullshit, and I will not tolerate it from anyone. I don't give a shit how many points you're putting up. I don't care how much you don't like your teammates. I don't give a rat's ass about what's going on in your personal life. When you're on my ice, you check your shit at the door. I gave you a pass the first time but I will not let you disrespect my game again. Do I make myself clear, son?"

I grind my teeth and give him a curt nod because deep down, I know he's right.

"Clear, Coach."

"Good. Now get the hell out of my sight." He looks at Lowell. "Get back out there."

Then he's gone, the door slamming shut behind him just like it did when he walked in.

"Fuck!" I shout, ripping my sweater over my head, throwing it across the room. "Son of a bitch!"

Lowell shakes his head, a disappointed frown marring his face. "I'll make sure Colter doesn't get off easy either."

"No," I tell him as I begin stripping my gear off. "You said it yourself, I instigated it."

He snorts, pushing off the bench. "Yeah, but the shit he said didn't make matters better."

He heads for the door, then hesitates.

"Hey, man, listen. If you need anyone to talk to…"

"You're there. Yeah, I know."

"Oh, you think I want to talk to you? No way. I was gonna put that shit on Rhodes. He's such a good listener and all."

For the first time in what feels like days, a smile tugs at my lips.

"And for what it's worth, I'm sorry it didn't work out with Harper. I really liked her."

Me too.

Instead, I swallow the lump in my throat and say, "Thanks, Lowell."

"Of course."

He disappears back down the tunnel, and I'm left in the dressing room feeling as defeated and broken as I did just six months ago.

The only thing worse than being on the ice losing is watching your team lose from the sidelines knowing you could be down there helping them.

"Fuck. This blows so much."

"Feel like an ass for letting your team down yet?"

I glare at Shep, who is sitting in the private team box beside me.

When I told him I wouldn't be playing tonight, he insisted on coming to keep me company. I think he just wanted to make sure I wasn't going to jump from the box or something.

"I really hate you sometimes," I tell him.

He just laughs, not giving a shit at all.

The second period winds down, and I cringe when I look at the scoreboard. It's 3-0, and with the way they're playing, I can't see how it's going to get any better.

As Lowell promised, Colter's out tonight too. I think it might have more to do with how swollen his eyes are, but still.

"So," Shep says, "you ever going to tell me what happened?"

"I told you. Got into it with Colter. Coach wasn't happy. The end."

"Right. Sure. And the reason you got into it with him was…"

I shrug. "You've met the guy. You tell me."

Shep laughs. "Fair enough."

He folds his hand over his stomach, stretching his legs out in front of him. He purses his lips, looking around the swanky box, whistling a soft tune that's getting on my nerves more and more by the second.

I ignore it.

He gets louder.

"Fuck, man." I throw my hands in the air. "Enough, okay? I'll tell you."

He grins victoriously and waits for me to spill all the sordid details.

"There's not much to tell. I was seeing a girl and—"

"The one who had you all smiley and shit?"

"Yeah." I clear my throat, trying to keep all emotion

out of my voice. "It didn't work out. We…uh…wanted different things."

I scratch at the beard I've been growing out the last week. And by growing it out, I mean I've been too fucking lazy to shave. What's the point? It's not like I'll be burying my face between thighs anytime soon.

"And?" Shep presses when I don't say anything else.

"And what?"

"That's it? That's the reason you're sitting up here tonight? Because some chick you were banging decided to move on?"

My eyes narrow at his choice of words, and slowly, Shep's brows rise higher and higher.

"Oh." He nods once. "You're in love with her."

I shift in my seat at his statement.

He sits up. "You're like really in love with her. And she doesn't love you back."

I toss my head back. "Yes, because that's just what I needed to hear right now."

"What happened?"

"What do you mean?"

"I mean, what happened? Why is she not reciprocating your feelings? Is it because your dick is small?"

"Fuck you," I mutter, and he chuckles. "No. It's actually because I'm too perfect."

His face screws up. "Say what?"

I explain to him what happened at the art show and

everything she said on the recording she doesn't know I heard.

When I'm finished, he doesn't say anything for a long time.

Then finally, he says, "This might not be what you want to hear, but I get where she's coming from."

"You do?"

"Yeah. I mean, she spent her whole life thinking her parents had this perfect marriage, and that was shattered in a big way. She's scared. Sometimes fear makes you do some really stupid shit."

"Why does it sound like you're talking from experience?"

He laughs somberly. "Because I am. Because I've been Harper before. I've pushed the people I love away because of fear, and I regret those years I missed every single day." He pats me on the back. "She'll come around."

"And if she doesn't?"

"Then you can either stay angry at the world and let it ruin everything you've worked hard for, or you can channel it into something big that weighs, oh, say, around thirty-five pounds." He lifts a brow. "You know what I'm saying?"

"I hear you."

Focus on the season. Don't let this get in my way.

"Good. But, Collin?"

I glance over at him and he's looking down at the ice, watching the Zamboni driver clean up.

"Real love doesn't come around often. Hell, sometimes it never comes around at all. But when it does…it's worth waiting for. Trust me."

For Harper?

I'd wait forever.

CHAPTER 22

"All right. I'm giving you until the count of ten to put away all of your creepy things, because I'm coming in."

I wish I were surprised that Ryan's standing at my studio door threatening to barge her way in, but since I haven't seen her in over a week now, I knew this day was coming.

"One!"

Crap. I really should take my spare key back.

"Two!"

I don't scramble to clean anything up, because for the first time in a long time, I have no desire to work on anything.

My work—my passion—is bringing me zero joy right now.

Nothing is, actually. Not my tried-and-true horror movies or my coffee bar or even a soak in the tub. Nothing feels good anymore, and I can pinpoint the exact moment when it began.

"Three!"

I rise from my stool and pull the door open.

"Ten," I say flatly.

"No, four. Did Count von Count teach you nothing?" she says, breezing into my studio.

I drop back onto my stool and pick up my paintbrush.

Not that I'm painting anything right now. I've been staring at this blank canvas since I got up this morning. And by got up, I mean since I peeled myself out of bed after a fitful three hours of slumber.

"Wow," Ryan says, coming to stand behind me. "It's beautiful. Really captures the emotion."

I don't know why, but something in her words triggers the floodgates, and tears begin to well up in my eyes.

"Oh, shit." She gathers me in her arms, hugging me closely. "I'm sorry. I didn't mean to make you cry."

She didn't mean to, but she lets me do it anyway.

I don't know how long we stand there with me sobbing into her shoulder, but it's long enough that eventually, the tears aren't coming anymore. All I'm doing is shaking.

Ryan directs me to the stool, then disappears for less than thirty seconds. When she comes back, she drapes a blanket over my shoulders and pulls it tight around me.

The minute I recognize it's the blanket I bought from the gas station during my mini road trip with Collin, I'm crying all over again.

When I finally get the tears to stop for a second time, I swipe angrily at my face.

"I don't even know why I'm crying. I'm the one who pushed him away. I'm the one who wanted this."

"That doesn't mean it's not going to hurt. Especially since you're in love with him."

I glower at her. "I am not."

She doesn't even try to hide her exasperation with me. "Yes, you are."

"I'm not, Ryan. I don't do love."

"You are, and I can prove it to you."

She disappears again, and this time I follow her. I curl onto the couch as she rummages through her bag, pulling out her laptop.

She clicks a bunch of buttons, and then a still-frame shot of me fills the screen.

It's from the art show.

"I just want you to know that the absolute *only* reason I listened to this is because you're my best friend and I needed to know how much I should brush up on my karate so I could kick Collin's ass for hurting you." A perfectly shaped brow quirks up. "But it turns out, it's your ass that needs kicked."

She hits play, and for several long seconds nothing happens.

Then there's a slight rustling, and I know it's Collin moving around with the recorder in his hand. He clears his throat.

"So."

It's one word—one silly, simple word—and already tears are threatening to spill over again.

"I guess we're supposed to send a message to the person on the other end of this thing, huh? Ryan said it could be silly or serious or something in between. I bet you're hoping I say the word *cunt*, aren't you?"

He chuckles, and the sound slides over me like a warm coat on a cold winter day.

"But I'm not going to. Well, shit. I guess I technically did, huh?"

Another low laugh.

"I have a confession to make. Last week when I got back from the game in Colorado, all I wanted to do was go home and sleep. So the second our plane landed, I was out and in my car with no time to spare. I got behind the wheel and I drove home. Only I didn't drive to my apartment. I drove to yours."

Just like it did the first time I heard it, his confession squeezes at my heart.

"At first I didn't understand it, so I just sat there in my car in your parking lot for a long time. Like way-past-the-level-of-appropriate kind of long. I kept trying to figure out why. Why? Why, when I was dead on my feet, when all I wanted was to go home, did I drive to you?" He sighs. "And then it hit me. It's because whenever I think of home now, I think of you. I think of you in bed, waiting for me to come crawling into the sheets after a game. I think of you lazing around in those ridiculous pajamas with the sexy Michael Myers on them. I mean, come on, what the hell even are those?"

"Rude," I mutter.

"That's not all I think about either, but I'm not going to say the rest on tape because I'm not so sure I trust Ryan won't ever listen to this."

"Smart man," the woman in question says.

"I think...I think what I'm trying to say is that maybe Lowell and Rhodes were right. Maybe the dick does protest too much and maybe there was a disturbance in the Force. And maybe...maybe I'm in love with you." He laughs dryly. "Oh, hell. Who am I kidding? There's no maybe. I am. I know it's not what we said we're doing and I understand if you're not here yet, but I couldn't come into this box knowing your reaction was going to be caught on camera and not tell you.

"So, Ryan, if you're listening...get ready to take the shot." A brief pause. "I love you, Harper. And I'll wait for you as long as you need."

The volume cuts out and the screen fades to black.

"Did you see it?" Ryan asks.

"See what?"

"Your face—did you see it?"

I shake my head. I wasn't paying attention.

Ryan hits rewind, then presses play.

"I love you, Harper," Collin says again.

"Did you see? Watch your eyes. Watch what happens when he says it."

She goes back again, hits play.

This time, I do what she says.

And this time, I see it.

"The way your eyes completely change...the light

that blinks into them and slowly transforms your face... that's what the project is about, capturing that raw emotion." She points at the screen. "That proves to me that you're in love with him too."

I'd be an idiot to try to sit here and lie to her, to tell her I'm not in love with Collin. But...

"I don't know if I can do it," I tell her.

"Why not? Because of your dad?"

"Yes. You know that."

"I do know that. Just like I know it's a bullshit reason."

"He cheated on my mother! He died—*died*—because he was cheating on her! She gave everything to him and he left her broken and he left me. He left *me* broken."

"I know he hurt you. I understand that. But you can't hide from everything just because you're afraid of getting hurt again."

"I can too."

"Fine. You can. But you're going to live a shitty life and you're going to miss out on a lot. Don't you find it ironic that you love horror movies but you're too scared to fall in love?"

"Horror movies are predictable. Love isn't."

"That's half the fun in it! Taking risks, putting yourself out there. That's the whole point."

"But if it fails?"

"Then it fails. And it hurts and it sucks. But you dust yourself off and you move on. Honestly, if someone told me falling in love was going to be a breeze and there would never be any kind of trouble or problems, I probably wouldn't want to fall in love."

"You wouldn't?"

"No. I mean, come on. Even romantic comedies have some sort of drama to them. It'd be boring if they just fell in love and that was it. There would be no...pizzazz, you know?"

I guess I can see where she's coming from, but...

"I'm scared."

"I know you are. But he's not like your dad."

"I know that."

"Do you?"

"Yes! But it doesn't make me any less scared to love him. What if I lose him too?"

"Haven't you already though? Wouldn't you rather love him fiercely while you can than not at all?"

I don't have to think about the answer to that question because it's a resounding *yes*.

I'd rather have some time with him than none at all, and I thought that was what I was doing by keeping it casual. We were together, but there was no risk involved.

I was a fool to think there was no way I'd fall for him.

How could I not?

"What am I supposed to do now?"

"Oh." She taps her fingers together excitedly. "I am so glad you asked. I have an idea..."

CHAPTER 23

"Well, J.P., I am telling you, there's just something different in the air tonight. Maybe it's having Collin Wright back out on the ice after being a healthy scratch last game, or maybe it's something else entirely. Either way, I've got a feeling this is going to be a good one."

"No doubt about it, Hank," J.P. agrees. "We have a packed house tonight too. The fans are excited and buzzing. I see a bunch of signs out there this evening."

"So many signs. There's even one with a special message for our returning defenseman it looks like. What's that say, J.P.?"

"*Hey, #96! You could say I'm a fan.*"

"Well, simple and to the point. We're all fans of #96. Here's hoping he can get back on that point streak tonight."

CHAPTER 24

"Say, did you catch the Carolina game the other night, Mikey?"

"I did. And if you're getting at what I think you are, that girl held that sign up all night long, Jonesy."

"Interviewers asked Collin Wright after the game what he thought and he opted to not answer, which led many to speculate about whether he knew the woman or not."

"Hmm, interesting. Oh, wait, hang on here. I think we have another Sign Girl tonight. No, wait. There are two! Hey, Jobe, can you get that camera over in Section 217?"

"Well, I'll be. We do! We have one tonight, Mikey! Looks like Collin Wright might have his very own fan club following him around."

"What's it say tonight, Jonesy?"

"*Hey, #96! You know what they say about tall hockey players, right?* And the other one reads, *Big sticks!*"

"Oh, thank god. Thought we were about to be in trouble on network television for a moment there, Jonesy."

CHAPTER 25

CHICAGO
AT CAROLINA

"We are back tonight with another Carolina Comets game, and I gotta say, this #SignGirlGate has taken the internet by storm, Mikey."

"I'm kind of hoping we have one here tonight. I'm invested."

"When Collin was asked about the latest sign last night, he laughed but didn't provide any more insight."

"I get the feeling he knows more than he's letting on, Jonesy. Maybe it's all to drum up publicity for something?"

"I don't know, Mikey. Collin Wright is a notoriously private man. I can't imagine he'd be participating in this for attention."

"Well, looks like our wishes are being granted! I just got word there is yet *another* Sign Girl in the building tonight. Camera, can we get an eye on her?"

"Ah! There she is! What's it say tonight?"

"*Hey, #96!* And then there's just a picture of a corn dog."

"A corn dog? Why a corn dog?"

"I do not know, but I'm sure the internet is going to be buzzing trying to figure out who this girl is."

CHAPTER 26

"We asked Collin Wright last night what he thought about the corn dog, and he said he took it as a compliment."

"Did he elaborate on what it means?"

"No, but it seems like a good thing. Most of Twitter is claiming it alludes to something sexual. Speaking of...the sign tonight might be a little racy for television, Mikey."

"I'm not even sure we can show it. Oh, we can?"

"Oh, man. I'm blushing just reading it."

"What's it say, Jonesy?"

"*Hey, #96! Want to have Creme Pies and Ding Dongs together?* They taped a Little Debbie Oatmeal Creme Pie and a Hostess Ding Dong onto the sign."

"Looks like our Sign Girl is growing bolder."

"And bigger. She was trending on Twitter last night *and* this morning. If only we could get Collin Wright's insight into all of this. He's been tightlipped on the whole thing."

"At what point do we question if it's affecting his playing, Jonesy?"

"Affecting his playing? I think it's helping! He's put up a point per game, and the Comets are on a hot streak right now. Whoever this Sign Girl is, if she's a fan of the Comets, she better keep them coming!"

CHAPTER 27

"No way, you're totally Sign Girl, aren't you?" I turn to find the woman from the first game I attended sitting a few seats down again. "Like the original one, yeah?"

I hold my finger to my lips, and she laughs.

"Oh, man. We've been following you since the beginning. I have no idea how you're getting these signs all over these last two weeks, but it's been entertaining, that's for sure."

"Well, I'm glad. Delia, right?"

"Yes, you remembered!"

"Kind of easy for me. I'm a big *Beetlejuice* fan."

"That's fair." She turns toward me, leaning across the seat next to her. "So what's the story—you two dating or something?"

"Or something," I answer.

"Playing your cards close. I can respect that."

"It's a little complicated. I sort of screwed things up, and I'm trying to make up for it."

"Oh, trust me—I totally understand that. I almost

lost the best thing that happened to me too. But after a very well-thought-out goat heist, it all worked out in the end." She waves her hand like she didn't just drop a really juicy tidbit. "Anyway, what's the sign say tonight? Is this the one where you win him back?"

"I hope so."

"I hope so too. My brother-in-law is actually Collin's agent. He's a really great guy. We're big fans of his."

"Is he really?"

"Yep. Shep's a total shithead, but he's really great at what he does. Not that I'd ever tell him that."

"You know that girl I was here with last time?"

"Gorgeous blonde?"

"Yeah. She sold some photographs to Shep's wife."

"No." Delia's eyes widen. "You have no idea how obsessed I am with her work. I keep trying to steal Denver's pictures. What a small world!"

"It really is."

"All right. I have nachos, popcorn, a large fry—extra ranch, of course—and a large Coke to split," Delia's husband says, plopping down into the seat next to her.

"Oh thank god. Sustenance." She reaches for the food, shoving a handful of fries into her mouth all at once.

"Hey! I got those for my ranch."

I think he means he got ranch for his fries, but I'm not going to question it.

Delia holds out a bucket of popcorn to me. "Want some?"

"No, but thank you."

"If you change your mind, just let us know. Zach tends to go overboard on the snacks."

"Because you tend to hog them all," he grumbles.

I'm too nervous to eat right now. Hell, I've barely been able to stomach anything for the last few weeks. Ryan played my message to Collin back to me, and I'd had no idea he heard everything I said. It makes me sick that he might think he's not worth it for me.

The team is about to take the ice for warmups any minute now, and from where I'm sitting, there's a clear view to the bench across the way.

There's no way Collin will be able to miss me.

"Hey, what'd I miss?" Ryan drops into the seat next to me.

"Just me trying to hold my vomit down."

"Stop it. It'll be fine. He's going to love it."

"Are we sure? I've seen all of his post-game interviews. Every time they ask him about the signs, he changes the subject."

"No. Every time they ask him, his lips twitch and *then* he changes the subject. He likes it. Trust me."

The few people in their seats already start buzzing around us, and I pull my attention to the ice.

A player from the Comets smacks a bunch of pucks off the wall and then the skates hit the ice.

I know the minute Collin steps out.

Ugh. Even from the other side of the ice, he looks incredible.

It's been nearly three weeks since I've seen him. That's three weeks of pure agony. Three weeks of having to live with the fact that I'm a moron for ever letting myself think he wasn't worth it.

Because he is.

He's worth it all and more.

He stops in the middle of the ice, his head bent low, talking to Rhodes about something.

"Go!" Ryan hisses beside me. "Do it!"

On unsteady legs, I rise from my seat and head for the stairs.

I walk down the few steps until I've reached the glass. Then, with a steadying breath, I push my sign up against it.

I have no idea how long I hold it there. Seconds, maybe minutes. I don't keep track because all I can focus on is remembering to breathe.

There's a tap on the glass, and I stumble backward, dropping the sign.

Collin.

He's staring down at me with those green eyes I love so much.

He's not smiling…but he's not frowning either. He's just watching.

Unsure of what to do, I lift my hand and wave.

"Harper!" Ryan hisses from somewhere behind me.

And just like in his interview, Collin's lips twitch.

"I love you!" I shout, unable to hold it in any longer.

His eyes widen and he takes a surprised step back.

At least I hope it's a surprised step.

I hope that in the last few weeks, he hasn't changed his mind.

Someone calls his name, and he looks torn between wanting to stay and needing to go.

"Go," I tell him. "I'll wait for you as long as you need."

"Oh, god. My arms are getting so tired."

"Then drop the sign. Collin's already seen it."

"No! It's my thing—my brand. You should know that, Miss Social Media Guru."

"Ugh. Whatever. Some days I really just want to erase my Instagram. I—"

A collective gasp moves through the arena and people shoot to their feet, trying to see what's going on.

There's a player down, and without even seeing who it is, I know it's Collin.

"What happened?" I ask the person on the other side of me.

They shrug. "I don't know. I missed it. Looks hurt though."

I want to yell *Yeah, no shit he's hurt*, but I refrain.

I watch as team medics run onto the ice to check on him. He's still down, and I really don't like that he's still down.

Finally, after what feels like hours, with just over half

of the third period left to play, Collin is helped off the ice. He gives the crowd a thumbs-up as he's assisted down the tunnel.

I suck in a large gulp of air, realizing I was holding my breath.

"Hey, it's okay," Ryan reassures me, pulling me back down into my seat. "I'm sure he's fine. It's probably just precautionary. He walked off on his own and gave a thumbs-up. That's a really good sign."

I exhale sharply, then suck in another breath of air, trying to calm myself. My stomach is rolling and I think I may barf. I'd give anything right now to know he's okay.

The game resumes, and the minutes tick by so damn slowly.

"Excuse me? Miss Kelly?" There's a man with a very official-looking badge hanging around his neck leaning over me. "Could you come with me, please?"

I look at Ryan, and she just shrugs.

"I'll be right back," I tell her, handing her my sign. "What's this about?" I ask the gentleman as I follow him up the stairs.

"Mr. Wright wanted to see you. We don't usually do this, but since we're all such big Sign Girl fans…"

He doesn't say anything else as he leads me through a series of tunnels and doors until finally he pushes one open and there sits a battered-looking Collin.

He gives me a small grin when he sees me, and my feet carry me across the room on instinct.

I don't stop until I'm standing at his knees.

There's a large gash above his left brow, and it's obvious he's favoring the right side of his body.

"I look worse than I feel, I promise."

They're the first words he's said to me in weeks, and suddenly they're my favorite words in the world.

"What happened?"

He shrugs, then winces at the movement. "Took a funny hit and my helmet came loose. My head bounced off the ice when I went down."

"Are you going to be okay?"

"Yeah. I'm done for the night, but I'm okay. Nothing serious. Just sore."

"See, I told you all the ramming was an awful idea."

"I didn't hear you complaining."

I blush at his words.

A silence falls between us. I have so many words I want to fill it with, but I don't know where to start.

"Harper, I—"

"No," I interrupt. "I want to go first, okay?"

"Okay. But can you at least come here?"

He reaches out for me, and I step between his legs. He drops his forehead to mine, one hand on my waist, the other cradling my face.

He sighs the moment we make contact, and I feel the exact same way.

"You wanted to go first?" he asks.

I nod, then swallow. "I...I'm sorry. I messed up. I...I pushed you away. I got scared and I freaked. I didn't know how to handle the fact that whatever we had wasn't casual. Hell, I don't think it's ever been casual, really. I didn't know what to do with the fact that you loved me, didn't know how to accept that, how to allow it…" I lick my suddenly dry lips. "I…I lost my father when I was sixteen. We didn't find out until after he passed that he was unfaithful to my mother for years. We had no clue, and it hurt us deeply. It hurt *me* deeply. He was my best friend. We did everything together. He was the one who turned me on to horror. He was the one who encouraged me to pursue art. He was the one who believed in me. And he lied. Over and over again. Straight to my face. It hurt so much to know that. I've been torn between loving him and being angry at him for the last eight years."

I sigh, pulling back, looking up into his eyes. "But I'm tired of being mad. I'm tired of being scared. I'm tired of always waiting for the other shoe to drop because I can't trust anyone. I want to be happy. Bold. Brave. And I want to fall in love and live in the moment of it, not worry about how or when it'll fail. Being without you these last few weeks… It hurt so bad and I don't want to feel like that again."

I reach out, brushing a tentative finger over his fresh cut.

"I love you, Collin, and I think—" I shake my head. "No, I *know* you're worth it. Worth taking that risk for…if you'll let me."

He doesn't say anything for a long moment, and I worry that maybe I'm too late.

But then he finally speaks.

"You know, I think a part of me started falling for you the first time we met."

"Really? Was it my driving skills?"

He chuckles, then winces. "Yes. It was definitely that. And also the fact that you were just so...*cute*." I glare at him. "You were funny and different and I just really liked being around you." He shakes his head. "I should have known. Should have known it when you calmed the storm inside me then."

"You're welcome."

He grins, pulling me closer. "Can I say something without you freaking out on me?"

"Yes."

"I love you."

I sigh. "Say it again."

"I love you." He brushes his lips against mine. "I didn't mean to fall. You were just supposed to be a distraction, something to keep my mind off the game. And it worked, maybe a little too well. I just...I love you. So much."

"I love you too."

He kisses me slowly and softly and for so long I'm sure the game is long over by now.

When we finally pull apart, there's a permanent smile etched on my face.

"One more question," he says.

"What's that?"

"The signs all over the country...how'd you do it?"

"It was Ryan's idea. She used her social media following to find hockey fans, and it just worked."

"It really did. I think tonight's sign was my favorite though."

"Yeah?"

"Definitely." He nods. "Because I love you too."

EPILOGUE

COLLIN

I glance up at the jumbotron as I fly down the ice, the puck at the end of my stick.

We're tied in Game Seven with a minute and a half to go.

Just one goal. That's all we need.

We can do it. I know we can. I feel it in the air. In my bones. It's palpable. So damn close I can almost fucking taste it.

I pass to Rhodes and he plays with it a bit, watching the other skaters before zipping it back my way.

Twenty.

I line up my shot, watching the Vegas guys in my periphery.

Fifteen.

I wait for the screen.

Ten seconds.

I pull my arm back.

Eight.

And swing.

The puck hits the back of the net, and the buzzer sounds with just seconds to spare.

We won.

We fucking won.

Gloves and sticks and helmets fly into the air as body after body slams into the glass with me trapped in the middle.

I've never been so thrilled to have the wind knocked out of me before.

"Holy shit!" Rhodes yells, grabbing me in a hug when he finally pushes through the crowd. I've never seen him smile so damn big before. "We fucking did it! We did it!"

He gives me a shake, then skates off, hugging everyone he can get his hands on.

"Come here, you beautiful bastard!" Miller grabs me next, kissing the side of my head. "Fucking killed it!"

And finally, when my captain skates up to me, I'm choking back the tears. I stick my hand out to shake his, and he shoves it away and hauls me into him. He hugs me tight, patting me on the back.

"Proud of you," he says into my ear.

"You too."

Everyone skates around, hugging one another about four or five times each. The air is pure electricity at this point.

We gather together for photos, and the Cup is presented.

It's all so surreal, and I'll remember the moment for the rest of my life.

My parents each give me a hug, then my brother and his boyfriend. When we're all hugged out, that's when I hear it.

"Hey, Hockey Guy!"

I spin toward my favorite sound in the world.

Harper's standing a few feet away, one of those silly signs she's so popular for hanging between her fingertips, a smile plastered across her face.

I don't waste a moment, skating toward her and scooping her into my arms.

I slant my mouth over hers, kissing her until we're both breathless.

"Hi," I whisper against her lips, setting her back down on the ice.

"Hi," she says on a smile, then gives me another peck. "I'm so proud of you."

"I couldn't have done it without you."

"I doubt that."

"It's true. You're my good luck charm."

"You don't really believe in all that mumbo jumbo."

I didn't, not really. Not before her.

"So, what's your sign say tonight?"

She pulls it out from behind her back and holds it up for me to read.

Hey, #96! I asked Lord Stanley if he wants to have a threesome tonight. He said yes.

"Hmm. Very fitting."

"How so?"

"Just something I've been thinking about lately is all."

Her eyes light up in surprise. "Oh, really?"

"Yep. Does that scare you?"

"Yes. Horribly so."

"My little Horror Harper. She'll fight off a killer or slay a demon, but when it comes to the man who loves her asking for her hand in marriage, she'll say—"

"Yes." Harper grabs my sweater, pulling me down to her. "She'll say yes."

"Really?"

She nods with a grin. "Really."

"Hmm. I'll have to keep that in mind." I kiss her again. "What if we had lost?"

"You wouldn't have."

"But you had a sign made anyway, didn't you?"

She nods, then pulls away and shows me other side of the sign.

A laugh bursts out of me as I read it.

Oops?

Shaking my head, I pull her back to me. "I love you, Harper."

She sighs against me. "And I love you, Hockey Guy."

Turns out getting the game-winning goal in Game Seven of the Stanley Cup Finals is a pretty damn good reason for your team to re-sign you for six more years.

I'm staying in North Carolina.

And that's why we're here in Vegas to celebrate. Well, that and the Cup.

"To Hot Hockey Guy!" an inebriated Ryan yells. "And Hot Hitchhiker!" She holds up what I think is her sixth shot...of the hour. That doesn't include the frozen drink she sucked down and the three shots she did before we even left the hotel. "He got the Cup, he got the girl, and he got the contract, baby!"

She downs the shot, not bothering to wait for anyone else.

I pull Harper into me, dropping my lips to her ear. "Your friend is completely hammered."

"Oh, I know."

"Think we should call it a night?"

"For all of us?"

She looks up at me with hope in her eyes, and I laugh. "Not so fast. I still have plans to dance with you tonight. I meant for the drunk one."

"Oh. Then my answer is still yes." She glances over at Rhodes, who looks like he's having the worst time ever. "I have no idea where Miller and Lowell ran off to, but think Rhodes can take her back to her room?"

Do I think so? Yeah. I trust Rhodes with my life. He'd never let anything happen to Ryan.

I kick his foot with mine. He directs his furrowed brows my way, and I slide my eyes up to Ryan.

Being Rhodes, he understands what I'm asking.

Take care of her.

He rises from the plush lounge chair and reaches up, grabbing Ryan down from the top of the booth where she's currently yelling and dancing.

"No, thank you!" she says to him, booping him on the nose.

His scowl deepens, and I can't help but laugh.

Annoyed, he slings her over his shoulder.

"Hey! You cranky hot giant! Put me down!"

He ignores her.

"Harper! Help!"

Harper just shakes her head. "No! Go lie down—you're drunk!"

Ryan gasps. "I am not!"

"Are too!"

"You traitor!" she yells to her friend, banging on Rhodes' back. "I thought you loved me!"

"I do!" Harper tells her. "It's for your own good."

"He's going to kidnap me and hold me hostage in his castle!"

I swear I hear Rhodes mutter, "You wish."

Ryan swats at him again, then shakes her tiny fist at us, and we laugh.

When they're out of eyesight, I grab Harper's drink from her hand, then stand. She looks up at me with confusion.

"Dance with me."

"No way."

"Harper Dolores Kelly…dance with me, dammit."

She laughs at the use of her full name and pushes to

her feet. I let my eyes trail over her body in a very appreciative manner. She's wearing a black dress that's full of sparkles, and it's hugging every damn curve she has. I already can't wait to see how it looks on our hotel room floor.

I pull her through the club and onto the dance floor. I don't go too far into the crowd, wanting to make sure she has a clear exit in case she wants to leave, but just enough that it feels like we're in a sea of bodies.

I tug her close to me, pressing my body against hers. I place a hand on the small of her back and bring the other up to my chest.

"Are you slow dancing with me in the middle of a club?" She grins up at me.

"Yes."

"Why?"

"I'm practicing," I tell her.

"For what?"

I pull her closer, dropping my lips to her ear. "Our wedding."

When I pull back, her jaw is dropped, and she's watching me with a surprised grin.

"What?" I ask, spinning us, not caring at all that we look like fools right now. "I'm being serious."

"I know you are." She shakes her head. "You're awfully full of yourself, Hockey Guy."

"Nah. I'm just sure I'm going to love you forever."

Her breath hitches and I watch her closely, waiting for her to freak out or say something.

She doesn't do either.

Instead, she presses her mouth to mine and tells me she feels the same with her kiss.

Thank you for reading **PUCK SHY**!
I hope you enjoyed Collin & Harper's story.

Want more Carolina Comets?
BLIND PASS is now available!

OTHER TITLES BY TEAGAN HUNTER

TEXTING SERIES

Let's Get Textual

I Wanna Text You Up

Can't Text This

Text Me Baby One More Time

INTERCONNECTED STANDALONES

We Are the Stars

If You Say So

HERE'S TO SERIES

Here's to Tomorrow

Here's to Yesterday

Here's to Forever: A Novella

Here's to Now

Want to be part of a fun reader group, gain access to exclusive content and giveaways, and get to know me more?

Join Teagan's Tidbits on Facebook!

Want to stay on top of my new releases?

www.teaganhunterwrites.com/newsletter

ACKNOWLEDGMENTS

The Marine. I love you.

Laurie. You're my glue.

My editing team. Caitlin, Julia, Judy…thank you ladies so much! You are the best to work with. I can't imagine doing this author thing without you.

#soulmate. You're always there, and I love you for that.

My mom and sisters. Thanks for always being there when I need a good laugh.

The game of hockey. I can't believe I haven't known you my entire life. Can't believe it took me so long to become an avid fan. I don't know what I'd do without you. It's safe to say you were my missing piece all along.

Tidbits. Thank you for always being there for me even when I disappear on you. I always feel your love.

Reader. I couldn't do this without you. Thank you for taking the chance on my first ever hockey romance. I'm excited to be diving into this new sub-genre and I truly hope you're excited for more Carolina Comets.

With love and unwavering gratitude,
     Teagan

TEAGAN HUNTER is a Missouri-raised gal, but currently lives in South Carolina with her Marine veteran husband, where she spends her days begging him for a cat. She survives off of coffee, pizza, and sarcasm. When not writing, you can find her binge-watching *Supernatural* or *One Tree Hill*. She enjoys cold weather, buys more paperbacks than she'll ever read, and never says no to brownies.

www.teaganhunterwrites.com

9 781959 194903